Born in Hertfordshire in 19~~ ~~ growing up in ~~~~on being regenerated in the early post-war years, author George developed a passion for writing historical events at an early age. After retiring from a busy business life and travelling to many countries from 1977 to 2015, he finally found time to write his first novel, *The Film*, ambition achieved.

Married to Jan since 1970, he has two sons and a daughter and now lives in Essex.

Essex County Council

To all the brave men and women who lost their lives during the First World War and the Second World War.
Also to my loving family.

George Amos

THE FILM

AUSTIN MACAULEY PUBLISHERS™

LONDON • CAMBRIDGE • NEW YORK • SHARJAH

A CIP catalogue record for this title is available from the British Library.

ISBN 9781788788618 (Paperback)
ISBN 9781788788625 (E-Book)

www.austinmacauley.com

First Published (2019)
Austin Macauley Publishers Ltd
25 Canada Square
Canary Wharf
London
E14 5LQ

Preface

Significant wartime events have not been included in this novel and have been omitted due to the time frame. It is not in any way meant to diminish the valiant and courageous efforts and successes of actual campaigns by the Allied Forces, such as the Battle of Britain, the rescue of the British Expeditionary Force at Dunkirk, the victories of the Eighth Army in North Africa, and the campaigns in Italy. There are so many other events that deserve merit; however, they are too numerous to mention in this short fictional work.

Introduction

It was one of the darkest periods in British history. The Second World War, destined to become a global conflict, had almost reached the shores of the British Isles. With Britain teetering on the brink of defeat, and German forces preparing to invade, the nation stood alone, determined not to surrender. The fictional events of this story could have been real, had it not been for the courage and sacrifice of the RAF pilots during the Battle of Britain. Hitler was forced to abandon his invasion plans codenamed *Sea Lion* following the failed attempt of Göring's Luftwaffe to gain air superiority, and his strategy to 'eliminate the English motherland' came to an inglorious end.

Chapter 1

On 14th May 1940, the people of the British Isles faced a catastrophic event. Not for a thousand years had the indigenous people of Britain been subjected to the humiliation of being subjugated by a foreign power. The British Expeditionary Force—defeated in northern France and Dunkirk—surrendered to the military might of the German forces, and Britain would soon be annexed by the tyrannical regime of Adolf Hitler. The Phoney War had ended, and with little remaining air and naval forces to defend the coast of England, Britain was at the mercy of the Axis power.

The Groves family had cherished their way of life. It was simple and uncomplicated, and their teenage children were healthy, polite and content. All this was about to take a sinister turn because of the Nazis, and their lives would change forever.

John and Mary Groves had lived in their family house since John inherited the property and his carpentry business from his parents. The house, situated on a quiet, cobblestoned road in Bethnal Green, was a small Victorian terrace with two small bedrooms, a scullery and a living room featuring a fireplace and hearth. When burning with coal, it was cosy and inviting and always something to look forward to after a hard day's work.

The brown-painted, wooden front door led directly on to the street and a small, highly polished step, which was often used during the warm weather to sit, chat and drink tea with neighbours. The house also had a cellar, common in many Victorian properties, which was used as a useful storeroom. John often thought of making it into another room, but Mary considered it to be somewhat damp, so she discouraged him.

At the rear of the house was a small backyard with a toilet, a coal hole and John's workshop, that was really a small shed. There was no hot water system, and washing and bathing were a lengthy business; they had to wait for an extremely large kettle to boil on the open fire. But it was their cherished home, and they had lived there since 1918.

Tension in the Groves's household was almost unbearable that summer morning in July; day after day, for a week, they had waited in their home, listening intently to the wireless and BBC News broadcasts. Unable to sleep well, they were tired and apprehensive, wondering what their fate would be when the Germans eventually arrived in their district. The latest broadcast that they had heard two days ago contained the shocking news that Britain had surrendered to the German forces.

Mary had taken her annual leave at the hospital, while John had decided not to take on any more projects for a while as a self-employed carpenter. It was difficult to concentrate on anything other than the events in the news.

John was angry. "Why isn't BBC keeping us informed about the Nazis, Mary?"

Mary did not need to reply, the answer came soon after when the crackled voice of a man with a German accent began to speak in English over the airwaves. "People of Britain, you are now under the administration of the National Socialist German Workers' Party and must remain in your homes for your own safety until further notice." The warning was stark but carefully worded so as not to cause panic.

The Gestapo had seized control of the London broadcasting studios at Portland Place in central London, and were swift with their inevitable propaganda.

"The Nazis are close, Mary," said John as he moved to comfort his family.

John Groves was born in 1898. An enigmatic child, seemingly indifferent to normal pursuits that his friends enjoyed during their formative years, such as street football and the like, he was more interested in military battles that his father had told him about.

His favourite pastime was to play with his miniature lead soldiers that his father had acquired for him. Young John was fascinated by the bright crimson uniforms fastidiously painted on each model. They would be arranged to re-enact famous battle engagements during the Boer War at the turn of the century, and John would spend much of his spare time in his bedroom.

Attending the local school, John proved to be a bright pupil, passing exams with ease, and when he left school at fourteen years of age, he was ready to join his father's small business as an apprentice joiner.

When he was seventeen years old in 1915, he sought to volunteer to fight in the First World War after seeing a poster with a picture of Lord Kitchener urging men to join the army or the navy. His father, who had served as a professional soldier under the command of Kitchener during the campaigns in South Africa against the Boers fifteen years earlier, had advised his son not to volunteer.

"Son, I know you feel left behind while everybody around you seems to be eager to go to war, but I feel many young men are using this as a means to escape from the monotony of their humdrum work at the factories, and they see it as glamorous, wishing to be heroes. The adventure they seek does not exist, and many will die in France just as they did back in my day in South Africa or will suffer injuries. I will not stop you, but take heed of my advice and wait, for the least amount of time you are at the front, the more likely you are to survive.

"Lord Kitchener has already made it public that conscription may be necessary early next year as volunteers alone will be insufficient to win this war. John, you have a good job working with me, and someday you will take over the business and run it yourself, so only go to France if you are conscripted."

The advice of John's father was sound and accurate, and conscription was introduced the following year.

After being conscripted, in January of 1916, followed by a brief training period, John was sent to France on the front line. Shocked by the terrible injuries and loss of men killed in action, he yearned for some normality even for a brief moment. He wrote home:

Dear Mum and Dad,

I hope my letter finds you both well.
I am really glad I did not volunteer like you advised me, Dad, as it is very difficult to be here. Some of my mates volunteered and have regrets as the war is not what they expected, and they have been here much longer than I.
We are all living in foul trenches twenty-four hours each day with terrible food—I miss your cooking, Mum, very much. Dad, I miss working with you a lot. Have you been to the doctor about your cough, like you promised?
Each day gets harder, but I am a strong person and will survive all the things they throw at me. I really am not frightened by any of it, so please don't worry about me, and our sergeant says the war will be over soon and we can all get back to our homes.
I miss you both very much and love you.

Your loving son,
John.

Two weeks after writing, John sustained his own tragic injury. It occurred when a piece of shrapnel hit the right side of his face as he was about to 'go over the top'. John's injuries were considered so severe, so he was evacuated from the trenches and sent back immediately to England where he became a patient at the famous Cambridge Military Hospital at Aldershot in Hampshire.

John was treated for two years at the hospital. That included plastic surgery on his disfigured face. It was a long and painful process, and nothing could save John's right eye.

The hospital, famous for its pioneering work in plastic surgery and shell shock victims, eventually sent John for convalescence to the Bethnal Green Military Hospital, and during his time there he met his wife-to-be and the future mother of his children. She was working as a trainee nurse and was an attractive young lady with brown eyes and long dark-brown hair tied in a topknot with a hat and a pin. John was immediately smitten by her. "Like an angel from heaven," he remarked to a patient in the next bed.

Mary, initiated into severe disability and suffering of injured soldiers from 1915, befriended John soon after he was admitted in 1918, and they were married at Bethnal Green register office on 26th December 1918, following his discharge from the hospital many months after his rehabilitation.

It was a time of severe austerity; the world war had been raging for four years and had taken its toll. The British Empire alone had sustained losses of nearly a million military personnel during the deadliest conflicts in history. Mercifully, it came to an end on 11th November 1918.

The marriage was a simple service, and the celebration afterwards was at home with just their family. Mary as a young girl had always dreamt of being married in a church, wearing a beautiful dress, but circumstances made that impossible.

Having a family was important to her and John, and after nearly four years of marriage, they were blessed with the birth of twins on 5th December 1922, naming them Mary Anne and James, after John's father.

Mary, also born in Hackney in 1898, attended school and left at the age of fourteen to pursue a career in nursing. Bright and enthusiastic, she gained qualifications to allow her to study at a nursing college at the local hospital in Bethnal Green.

As a student nurse, Mary had been advised by a senior nurse not to form attachments to the injured soldiers during their treatment at the hospital and was told it was unprofessional. Mary, however, was immensely impressed by John's courage and will to get better. He was also showing signs of being shell-shocked and was, at times, deeply distressed about his scars and the prospect of wearing an eye patch for the rest of his life.

Mary was sympathetic and caring and, with much patience, was able to help John to rehabilitate quicker. His confidence grew, and he became less conscious of his disfigurement. Spending so much time together, the friendship developed into romance. Nearly two decades later, however, their whole life had been turned upside-down by the gravity of the situation.

"What will become of us, John?" asked Mary.

"I hope the Germans will allow us to carry on with our lives as normal, but try not to worry," John replied, trying to console his wife, but he knew things would never be the same again after the Germans had annexed the whole of the British Isles.

There was no escape from the infamy of the Gestapo and the SS. They had both listened to the warnings and prophecies of Mr Churchill.

"If only the government had listened many years ago, maybe we would not be in this position," John said angrily. "The bloody pacifists who sought to appease a madman like Hitler are responsible for this, and now we are all going to suffer the consequences."

John was still furious, and Mary pleaded with him not to say any more in front of the twins as she could see Mary Anne was becoming upset. James, however, was calm and unresponsive; his temperament was like his father's.

John and Mary had seen in the newsreels, at their local cinema, how the SS had persecuted the Jews in Germany, Poland and France, and knew how ruthless the Nazis could be. Their concerns were for the twins. *Their safety is paramount,* John thought.

"What should we do?" asked Mary, becoming very impatient and agitated.

John had now calmed down, thankfully, and replied, "At the moment, we must stay indoors and listen to the wireless and await instructions from the Germans, unfortunately." John, who had some experience from the First World War, knew of how tenacious and organised the Huns could be.

John was distinctive, and was fully aware of how people stared at him, but in time, he became okay with wearing the leather eye patch. After all, it hid some of his scarred face, and wearing a glass eye was messy and unsightly; it made him recognisable and remembered.

John was indeed unforgettable to all, particularly the locals. He was always enthusiastically willing to help others in need. Mary, being a nurse, was often asked to assist people who were unwell and the twins were well liked in the area, and attended the local school. They were a well-respected family. They knew that many would be knocking on their door, seeking advice.

John's parents were now deceased, and he had no siblings; however, Mary's were both alive and living quite close. Peter, her father, and her mother—also called Mary—were a typical London family, born and bred in Hackney. Peter would often boast, "I'm a true cockney and proud to be one." He was also very proud of his daughter that she was a nurse and highly respected in the neighbourhood. Mary also had a younger sister named Elizabeth, whom she called Liz, living with her parents.

It had only been a few hours since the German broadcast, and now the terrifying moment had arrived—the Germans were in the street.

"John, please get Mum, Dad and Liz. I am worried about them," Mary requested anxiously.

Without warning, a loud noise was heard outside their house, and they could hear shouting distinctively in German. The invaders had arrived, and fully armed soldiers were fling in outside on the street. Then came another lorry, and then another; soon, approximately a hundred soldiers had amassed and sealed off the road.

"It is too late to get your parents, Mary. I'm sure they will be okay, and I'll fetch them later," said John, trying his best not to sound worried. Soon the Germans would be knocking on their door, he knew, and the family braced themselves for the inevitable.

Chapter 2

Outside the Groves's house, there appeared SS officers, easily identified by their black uniforms and Luger pistols. They were giving orders to other men that appeared to be ordinary German Army personnel. The SS was feared by everybody, including Wehrmacht soldiers. Then came a loud knock on the Groves's door and the terrifying shout commanding them to open immediately.

John, though worried, obeyed and opened the front door, while the other members of the family moved nervously to the scullery. James wanted to stay with his father, but John had insisted he must be with his mother and sister in the scullery.

The SS men pushed John aside and went straight into the back and dragged Mary and the twins back into the front room and forced them all, including John, against a wall at gunpoint.

"We want to see your papers, and you must tell us if you are Jewish," commanded one of the officers.

John was so tense and worried for his family that he could hardly speak. "We have no papers and are not Jewish. We do not have identity documents in this country," he uttered.

"Are there any Jewish people living in this street?" the SS officer asked abruptly while indicating to another SS man to search the house.

John knew of a family about six doors away that were. However, his reply was, "Not to my knowledge." As he knew their fate if he had told the truth.

"Stay in this house, and do not come out!" the German shouted in an angry fashion to assert his authority. Then they left.

It had been a frightening ordeal, and the family huddled together, with Mary being the first to speak up. "Will they come back, do you think, John?"

"No, I don't think so. Their priority is to round up all Jews first, I'm sure," John replied.

Mary then did what all British people would do in a crisis—she put the kettle on to make tea. But she was still shaking in fear. John knew that his wife was trying to ease the tension by acting normally for the sake of the family; they both knew that they would receive another visit soon.

As dusk fell that day, Mary's growing concern was for her parents and sister. She had not seen them since the Germans arrived, and, normally, day visits were made to see if they were okay. There was a terrible feeling of desperation within the family since the intrusion of the SS officers into their house. They had lived there for twenty-two years. It was their home, and they were now insecure, not knowing what would happen next.

Two hours had passed and, at Mary's insistence, John tentatively opened the door of their house and ventured out to fetch Mary's parents. The street was quiet, and the Germans had left the area, so John quickly moved to bring them back to Mary. She was so happy to see them, and that they were shaken but okay. It was an emotional reunion, and Mary suggested they stay overnight.

"Mother, I will feel happier if you are here with us."

Surprisingly, the elder couple seemed unaffected, but Mary's sister was distraught and difficult to console. It would be a long night for everyone, and sleep would be difficult, probably impossible. Mary was anxious and wanted to know what the Germans had said to them before the family retired to bed.

"Two men in dark uniforms, armed to the teeth, burst into our house and asked if we were Jewish. I told them right away that we were Protestant people, and they left. They were very rude," replied Mary's mother.

"They asked us the same question as well, but Mother, you must be very careful with these people and not argue with them. They can be cruel and sadistic." Liz was relieved to be with her sister and felt much better. Mary was always the stronger of the two even when they were young girls.

The next morning was bright and sunny, and Mary cooked some breakfast. Her parents had slept downstairs on the sofa and Liz on a mattress laid alongside. Some normality in their lives—even for a short time—made them all feel happier, and not seeing the soldiers in the street was reassuring.

John looked tired and had spent most of the night thinking of his own parents, who were fiercely patriotic, and what they would have thought about this current scenario. They both died of consumption during the early 1920s.

His parents had worked hard all their lives and had been subjected to living with the pollution and smoke of London's East End. The poverty and filth in the streets during Victorian times was appalling, and many had been destined to an early grave. John was proud and respected his parents, and was amazed that they were able to buy their own house with the money they had saved.

"The Industrial Revolution had created great wealth for some, but most did not share in the prosperity, and only suffered from the effects of the pollution." John always pointed this out to his friends. He was not a communist, but he had strong views about how unfair society was because of his own background.

The next morning, John took Mary's family back to their own house. John was relieved since the Groves's household, with only two small bedrooms, was very crowded when Mary's family stayed overnight. It was difficult to accommodate them and inconvenient to have everybody staying in such a small space.

But this is an emergency, John thought.

Chapter 3

Will we be treated the same as our European neighbour France, and how will this affect the rest of the empire? John thought.

The royal family and the prime minister, and most of the cabinet had been evacuated to Washington in America several weeks before the invasion, where they would be safe. The British nation, with their special relationship, would now be looking towards that country for their salvation, and possibly to the East, namely Russia. But it was on its ally America, the most powerful and richest country, that their forlorn hopes depended.

The militarist Japanese government was hostile to America and posed a threat to the Pacific region, as well as the whole of South East Asia. The Greater East Asia Co-Prosperity Sphere, instigated in 1940, was really a policy designed to subjugate and dominate other nations in Asia and the Pacific Ocean. The Americans had not entered the war yet, but watched, deeply concerned about Japan's military ambitions.

It had been a month since the arrival of the Germans. The family was looking at their immediate problems and surviving as best they could, facing an unknown future. Mary thought that maintaining food and water was the top priority, but to John, the most important was trying to keep the Germans away from their house or finding a hiding place for the twins and their mother.

The house, with its cellar, can provide us with a hiding place, John thought.

"Mary, I'll have a look in the cellar to see if there is a place to hide for you and the rest of the family, and then we can see if the grocery shop is open for supplies. We must act urgently before the Nazis come back to the street." John was in a fervour to ensure the safety of his family.

"John, I think I will need several visits to the shop, and our neighbours will also be anxious to stock up. The Nazis will start rationing soon, and we must get all we can. It doesn't sound fair, I know, but we are in a war situation."

"I'm okay with that. We have not been able to get petrol since the British government introduced the rationing last year before the Germans invaded," replied John.

The shop was open, and many local residents were there, buying what they thought was needed. Mary was quick to purchase whatever she could and then returned to the house, while John was busy sorting out somewhere safe to hide in the cellar. His joinery skills came to good use when he immediately started to build a false wall and cavity from wood, obtained from the workshop in the backyard.

Mary, also, was resourceful and knew exactly what they would need: bandages, medicines and many foods that were imperishable, such as tinned and dried foods. Her skills as a nurse were equally important. In fact, the whole family— including her parents, sister and the twins—were put to work. It was a great way to take their minds off the imminent return of the Nazis and the possible dangers they were facing.

It took John a few days to finish his work in the cellar with help from his son, James, and his father-in-law, and after building a secret access to the cellar to conceal the entrance from the ground floor, a trap door was made that would be covered by a rug and a sofa. The normal cellar entrance and staircase were left so as not to look suspicious, and the false wall in the room was cleverly concealed by old wood to match the other walls. There was sufficient room, albeit cramped, to accommodate Mary's family and his own with space for supplies. John was delighted with his work.

When Mary saw the finished hiding place, she named it straight away as the Hide. She was so relieved and pleased that she could store food and water, and have a place to escape should the need arise, and she immediately took most of the supplies down there. Somehow it gave the family a little security, and they hoped it would not be discovered by the Germans.

"John, you have done an amazing job in such a short time," Mary said to acknowledge his work.

Now, it was time to wait. "Mary, we are ready for the Nazis when they return," John said. He was satisfied that he had done everything possible to keep his family safe.

Chapter 4

With the dark period of occupation, courage was beginning to emerge, and brave men and women started to talk of resistance against the Nazis. London, and indeed the whole country were making plans to form cells that would fight back against the Nazi invaders. Britain had learned lessons from the underground movements in other occupied countries, and secret plots were being discussed among ordinary citizens to sabotage or kill senior Nazi officers. John Groves was one such man.

John was anxious to see his friends in order to recruit members for a resistance movement. One of them was Bill Wright, a veteran from the Great War who had been decorated for bravery and had been conscripted with John. Their meeting had to be completely clandestine and behind closed doors since the Gestapo was suspicious of everyone. *What better place than the Hide*, John thought, *where they could talk freely and safely?* Bill, on arrival at John's home, was warmly greeted by John and Mary. Mary was pleased to see Bill was okay, and after tea, the two men descended to the basement. There was mutual trust between them, and both knew they could depend on each other.

Bill, a tall man in his early fifties, was pleased he could express his anger to his friend. "How can we suffer this humiliation, John? Fighting in the last war, I firmly believed my family and country would be safe forever."

"So did we all, Bill, and as the days go by, I become more frustrated not doing anything. We cannot sit back and let the Nazi scum take over our country without doing something." John was seething with anger inside, but it did help him to talk to Bill to vent some of his suppressed feelings.

"But what can we do?" asked Bill.

"I'm pretty sure there will be many resistance movements formed as they are in Europe. The British character will not allow us to do anything otherwise," replied John.

Bill then hastily replied, "I will join in and fight back—however dangerous it is."

John was more cautious and preferred to wait before making any rash statements and immediately thought of his wife and children if anything were to happen to him.

"I hear the Nazi scum have taken away all the Jews from Whitechapel and Mr and Mrs Jacobs from number 14, a harmless elderly couple who have lived in this street for thirty-odd years," Bill retorted angrily.

"The Nazis will be back soon, and then we will talk again, Bill, and see what the situation is then." John was reticent to commit himself too much at this stage, but he knew in his heart that doing nothing was not an option. "Bill, I must tell Mary some of our plans. It would be extremely dangerous for us and, possibly, our families. You should discuss yours with Kim as well before we make definite plans," said John.

"You are right, John. I will discuss it with my wife tonight," answered Bill, and he left.

As the weeks went by, John and Mary tried their best to act normally. Mary travelled to work at the hospital, and John always went with her and then took the twins to their respective places of work. James was employed as an assistant rounds man for the local dairy company, and Mary Anne was working at the hospital with her mother as a part-time trainee cook in the kitchens.

German soldiers in the streets of London and tanks that rumbled noisily on the roads designed for horses, became deafening at close quarters, and local people held their hands to their ears to mute the sound. As a show of strength, it was effective, but not as frightening as one would imagine. There was always that nagging feeling, however, that the Germans would create more problems for the British public when they were more established, and this worried the population of London, including John and Mary.

It had taken just six weeks to put in place a Nazi administration and de facto government, and by midsummer, England, Scotland and the whole of Wales were now part of the Third Reich enforced by Wehrmacht soldiers and the SS, with Gestapo operating covertly. Northern Ireland and the south would not be occupied immediately, and the Channel Islands, being the first part of Britain to be occupied, would remain so because of its strategic location. A small contingent of the Wehrmacht would be permanently based in Jersey and Guernsey.

So the annexation of the British Isles was now official, and Operation Sea Lion, as the invasion was so called, had succeeded. Adolf Hitler wasted no time to show his vanquished enemy that they were now part of the Third Reich with a fascist dictatorship in full control.

On 15th August 1940, Hitler entered London and, with several divisions of the Wehrmacht and his personal bodyguard of SS troops, paraded through the empty streets to the Buckingham Palace and then to the Houses of Parliament just as he had done in Paris.

Londoners had stayed away, unable to stomach the humiliation, and were happy when, after only two days, Hitler returned to Berlin. It had not been a visit of a conquering hero as he had envisaged many months ago but a hollow and undignified, embarrassing event.

When Hitler arrived in Paris with his tanks earlier that year to celebrate his victories in France, two million Parisians had already fled the city, so maybe Hitler was becoming accustomed to a less-than-cordial welcoming!

"Seriously though, it made me sick to my stomach to hear the German news about the visit of that fascist pig," John said scathingly to an equally angry Mary as they both listened to the propaganda on their wireless.

The Nazis propaganda news broadcast could be heard also on loudspeakers strategically placed around the city, so even if you did not have a wireless set or switched it off, the nauseating sound was inescapable and incessant.

"The führer wishes to express to the citizens of Britain and the Reich that he appreciates the welcome given to him during his recent visit to London—"

John was unable to listen to any more and switched the wireless off angrily, but he could still hear it outside the house.

Chapter 5

The Groves family were feeling more dejected each day and with good reason. Gradually, life in Hackney began to change, and the local people were subjected more often to interrogation in their streets and were constantly under the watchful eye of the German soldiers.

The jackboot was all around London and everywhere the goose-step marching of the German units was commonplace. Although children found this very entertaining and amusing to watch, it was, for the adult population, sinister and unnerving and difficult to stomach.

The Public House, a British institution for hundreds of years, was now filled with off-duty Wehrmacht soldiers, and the local people stayed away, not wanting to associate or be seen with the rowdy, drunken, intimidating enemy. The nightly curfew after 11 p.m. for all British inhabitants was an affront to public liberty and fast becoming intolerable.

The general public went about their business—as far as possible—in the usual way, and John and Mary and the twins did the best they could to have normal lives. But their anger festered, particularly with John, who had been having his promised secret meetings with Bill Wright to form a partisan movement in London, and they began planning their strategy.

It was a bold plan designed to disrupt services initially and sabotage the transportation of supplies and troops to and from the south coast. The plan B was to activate a more aggressive military option, should they join another movement. John was realistic and knew that it would take more than their plans to drive the Germans out of the British Isles, but at least it would make him feel better that he was doing something to help avenge his country; however, he worried constantly about the dangers of even harbouring such plans.

Chapter 6

The year 1940 had come to an end, and after a very miserable Xmas, the new year of 1941 started badly. Rationing of nearly all food and energy materials, such as coal, was now implemented by the German authorities, and the austerity measures were beginning to have an effect on everybody, especially the elderly and the infirm. Life in Britain was becoming more and more desperate and unpleasant.

The family was thankful that they had stored these precious commodities in the Hide for this very reason. The Germans were enforcing these regulations by entering homes, searching and confiscating whatever they could, but they never found anything in the Groves's home as a result of John's work in the basement in spite of several random visits.

Jews were allowed to initially be free as long as they wore a badge with the Star of David, but soon there was a sinister and terrifying change. Jewish businesses and shops were closed and vandalised by the SS, and they were rounded up along with gypsies and criminals destined to be transported to secret detention centres across Britain. Eventually, some would be deported to Poland; families were being separated in the most inhumane way. Himmler's new reign of terror for the Jews had begun just as it had across Europe, and the scourge of this most evil of Hitler's henchmen was horrifying.

The wireless broadcasts were still being completely controlled by the Gestapo, and newspapers were strictly censured.

"The British people are in the grip of terror and being ridiculed each day by the presence of the Nazi invaders," John said to Mary during another outburst of anger.

John had discussed with Mary his plans for partisan activities, and she had agreed on the condition that the twins and her family would be safe from retribution by the Gestapo. The twins were always her top priority, and she would sacrifice her own life to protect them.

Meanwhile, John and Bill had finalised their plans. They had tried to keep the party limited in number to reduce the risk of discovery by the Gestapo, but soon realised they needed help from other like-minded activists.

Bill had recruited two of his old railway work colleagues, Michael and Gordon; both had experience of railway tracks in there locality. John had approached another neighbour called Brian, who was eager to join their group. Their covert activities would only be secure by complete secrecy, and even their families would not know anything of their exact plans.

They had heard about French partisans being executed by the Gestapo in France and Holland because of careless conversations, and the plain-clothed Gestapo had infiltrated London like 'rats in the sewers' as John once described it. They were everywhere, listening and arresting any person or group behaving suspiciously, and many just disappeared.

John raised the question quietly with Bill. "Are these men trustworthy, Bill, and do they know that nothing can be discussed outside of these four walls, and that not even their families must know of our plans?"

"I have explained that to them, so it should be safe, but we must have help, John, to carry this plan through. Like you, I would prefer to work alone, but it just isn't possible," Bill replied.

Since the German soldiers and equipment were being transported from the coast, they decided on a plan to sabotage trains that were being used by the Nazis for their first action.

"Bill, is my plan feasible?" John enquired.

"Yes, it is, but we will need to find the right spot, and it must be level so that we can use the van to help move the dismantled tracks. They weigh a ton, but we do not need to move them much. You know, John, I think we can actually do it! Thank goodness the Germans have lifted the curfew now, so we can drive by night," Bill replied with a wry smile.

Bill's expertise with railway tracks would certainly be crucial as he knew how to dismantle the lines; he also had the equipment to do this. So, after darkness had descended, they collected John's old van from its usual parking area, and John drove it to Crawley in Sussex. The area was flat, and they could use the van to shift the tracks just enough so that a German supply train would be derailed.

"Hopefully killing some of the Nazis!" Bill said.

The five men dismantled two tracks from the main line. It was dangerous work, and they all laboured for many hours, each man was aware of the consequences if they were discovered. Torture and then death by firing squad were what they could expect, and their families would be in danger too. John again reminded everybody of the need for complete secrecy before they left to return to their homes. The deed was done, and there was no turning back. Strangely, the five men were remarkably calm, considering the dangers.

They arrived back in London in the early hours of the morning and were disappointed that they were unable to wait and watch the results of their labour, but John in his wisdom had insisted in not being around when the train crashed.

"It would be too dangerous for us," he said.

When John finally arrived home, he was careful not to tell Mary what he had done and prayed that he and the others had not been spotted. John, strangely, was not nervous that night. His feelings were of relief and satisfaction at having found a way to fight back against the Nazi regime; however, his anger remained unabated.

In the morning, the family had breakfast together. All was quiet outside, so Mary was relieved and hoping that this would be John's last participation in the resistance movement, but she knew in her heart that her husband had a stubborn streak and, in all probability, would not finish with the movement he had founded so faithfully. The twins and her family were unaware of the full events of the previous night, but had their suspicions.

The less they know, the better, thought Mary.

During that afternoon, the family walked to Bethnal Green at John's suggestion as he wanted in earnest to find information and results of their clandestine activities. As they walked past number 14, the home of Mr and Mrs Jacobs, they were shocked to see the word *Juden* painted in red on the front door. Mary Anne asked what it meant, and Mary translated it for her. "Jew," she said.

The house looked empty, and James said, "They were always nice to me when I was a boy. Where have they gone?"

"They have been taken away by the Germans, so we have to be careful," replied Mary tearfully.

As they approached the town hall, John was the first to notice a giant red swastika flag hanging and blowing in the breeze halfway up the front facade. This angered Mary's father. "I was born and bred in this town. How can it be there is a swastika here?" he said furiously.

As they looked at the front notice board, Mary became deeply shocked as they read the following: "The German high command in this area is fully aware of the partisan resistance. These activities and acts of treason will not be tolerated, and the perpetrators will be punished—by order of the German high command."

The message was clear, and it sent a shiver down Mary's spine. John's reaction was completely different, for he knew now that he and his fellow saboteurs had been successful. Inwardly, he was jubilant and could not wait to see Bill and the others to give them the news.

John's plan had worked and had sent a firm message to the German invaders that the British people would not just lie down and die, but would fight by whatever means they could.

When they all arrived back home, Mary's family went to their own house, while John, Mary and the twins looked into the Hide to take stock of their supplies. Everything had diminished considerably, and Mary firmly gave the order that they would all ration the food they was left.

Food and coal were hard to obtain, and long queues at every grocery shop prevailed all day. It was so bad that many waited the whole day to buy meagre rations that were not enough to feed even a small family, and domestic coal was virtually impossible to obtain.

During the last six months of a cold winter, the public burned their furniture to keep warm in extreme weather conditions. "We must all ration ourselves. Otherwise, the food will run out. You must all eat less, I'm afraid, and that includes my family—my parents and sister. When the next winter season comes, more of the furniture, or what's left, will have to be used as firewood. It is going to be a long winter," Mary had warned earlier.

Mary had maintained her job as a nurse and was very busy caring for an overwhelming number of patients, many suffering from malnutrition. A greater part of the food available was now being consumed by the German Army, and the shortages were rife across England and the unoccupied parts, such as Wales and Scotland. John's work had dried up, but he was more interested now in his other activities with his friend Bill.

Children, generally, were still attending their schools as usual, and this was encouraged by the German authorities. They were desperately trying to keep life as normal as possible to make the administration easier.

The warmer weather in the spring of 1941 lifted the spirits somewhat of London's beleaguered population; however, the food crisis still remained, and the Germans were implementing even more stringent measures to enable them to feed their occupying force.

Mary was angry. "Don't they realise that our people are already starving?" she said to John, who seemed passive about it as he had been thinking about the resistance movement's next sortie to hurt the Nazis.

Where and how the group would strike necessitated another meeting, and John was becoming more and more impatient with the worsening events. "Things will only get worse, Mary, until we rid the Nazis from our shores," John replied.

Chapter 7

It was a warm, sultry day on 21st April 1941. John was sitting on his favourite part of the sofa. Mary was at the hospital, and the twins were both at work, so it was a good time for John to think, relax and make plans for the resistance movement.

Suddenly, there was a loud banging on the front door, almost making the house shudder. Peering through the curtain, John saw two men and a large car outside, parked about twenty feet away from the front door. John knew at once that the two men were plain-clothed Gestapo, and the vehicle was a German Mercedes, with a swastika on the bonnet. He immediately assumed they were there to arrest him, and he began to sweat nervously, fearing that he would not see his family again.

Carefully opening the door, he nervously asked the men, "Who are you, and what is the purpose of your visit?"

After showing their identity badges, they replied, "We have brought a visitor to see you today. Please allow us to enter your home."

John was flabbergasted at their politeness. *So different from previous visits by the SS,* he thought. He then invited the two men to enter.

He was expecting to be interrogated and then taken somewhere to be tortured and executed. Instead, they were nervous, apologetic. They sat down calmly and began to explain the reason they were there. "In the vehicle outside is a distinguished and high-ranking officer of the Reich, and he wishes to talk with you. Please treat him with the highest respect, yah?"

"Okay," John replied, feeling so relieved that the visit was not for another reason.

One of the Gestapo men went outside to escort the officer into the house, and after greeting John with a 'Heil Hitler' salute, he started the conversation, "Allow me to introduce myself. I am

General Ludwig Graf Von Klaus and have travelled from Berlin to talk to you on an important matter." John was stunned.

The general was wearing an Iron Cross with many other military decorations and was obviously extremely high ranking. *So what would he want with me?* he thought.

"I am here to inform you that you have been randomly chosen with your family to play the leading role in a film—" the general was careful not to mention propaganda "—about our new acquisition of the British Empire. It is to be directed by Leni Ribbentrop, our first lady of film. Joseph Goebbels, our minister, has asked me to arrange for the film to be completed by the end of May this year, and this will require us to make preparations with great urgency."

John was unable to comprehend fully what the general was saying to him; it was all happening too fast.

"Please sit down, Herr Groves. I understand it is a shock for you, but it is also a great honour for you and your family," remarked the general.

John was aghast and bewildered that he was being ordered to appear in a film for the Nazis, but he realised it would be dangerous not to listen and that it could destroy his family. He began to speak to the general as best he could. "Why have you chosen us? We are just an ordinary family."

"That is the reason, Herr Groves. Your profile for this is perfect, it and will make your family wanting for nothing more as it will give you fame throughout the Third Reich. We have been studying you for many weeks, and the decision has been made," replied the general.

"Please give me a few moments to think," answered John, thinking that the Gestapo might know about the partisan movement. If they did, then extreme caution would be necessary.

The Nazi is saying that I cannot refuse in a roundabout way, so I have no other options. But of course, it will put me in a terrible position with my comrades and in conflict with my convictions and, most importantly, endanger my family, John thought.

The general then asked John about his eye patch.

31

"I lost my eye during the last war when I was eighteen years old," John replied, slightly embarrassed.

"Das ist gut, Heinz, sind sie einverstanden?" (That is good, Heinz. Do you agree?) said the general, turning around to speak with one of the Gestapo men.

"Ja, Herr General."

John did not speak any German, but he understood what was being said.

"Forgive me, Herr Groves. I don't wish to be flippant about your injuries. It's just that it makes you a hero of the last war, and that will be excellent for the film. What time will your wife and children be here as I should like to meet them, John? I would like in future to be less formal with you as we will be meeting many times."

"They will be here in an hour," John replied apprehensively. He was worried about Mary's reaction.

"Okay, John, we will wait. Do you have any wine so I can propose a toast to our new international stars?"

"No, only tea," replied John.

"I like tea, but we will ensure that, in future, you will have as much wine as you need and anything else. See to it, Heinz," the general stated firmly. "Make sure it is good, German white wine and French red." The German laughed.

Before Mary entered the house, she was aware all was not well. She had seen the big car outside and the driver dressed in uniform. As soon as she entered the front room, the general immediately stood and kissed Mary's hand and introduced himself. If nothing else, this man was an upper-class gentleman, and there were indications that he was a charmer, John observed.

"Please call me Ludwig, Mrs Groves, and I would prefer if you would allow me to call you Mary."

Then the twins arrived home, and the general commented about them, saying, "What a handsome family you have." It was a statement rather than a question. "I will leave you now as you have much to discuss. Heinz will stay with you for a while in case you have further questions, so I bid you good day, as the English say." The general then left.

Mary was still totally bewildered and demanded explanations from John, which he gave. They both knew that Heinz was really there to report back to the general so they had to be very careful of what was said. John then turned to Heinz and asked him who the general really was.

Heinz replied in reasonably good English, "Count Ludwig Von Klaus is one of the highest-ranking generals of the Wehrmacht and a favourite of our führer. I have the honour and privilege to serve him as—I think you say in English—a batman." It was a proud reply to the question.

"So he is a count, an aristocrat?"

"Yes. His ancestry is pure pedigree from Prussia," said Heinz. "I have served the general since 1934, and as long as you obey his orders, you will be looked after by him. He is an honourable man."

After one hour, a car parked outside, and Heinz said goodbye and left the house, but not before informing the Groves that he would return tomorrow.

At last, the family could talk openly now about their situation, and that included the twins. John explained that they were in a very difficult situation. "If we refuse to take part in this propaganda film, we will be in danger from the Gestapo. On the other hand, if we do, we will be treated by our own friends and maybe our family as collaborators with Germany. It is a dilemma, Mary. The most danger for us at the moment is from the Nazis, so I think we should agree to appear in the film. At least, we will be protected by the Germans and rich enough to live anywhere in the world."

James seemed excited about the prospect and stated he would like to be a film star. Mary Anne was less enthusiastic and stated she would be nervous to appear in front of so many people.

Mary was surprised that her family were so quick to make decisions and said, "Do you all realise how it would affect our lives? These people are our enemies."

John was quick to reply, "Mary, we have no choice. The consequences, should we refuse, would be suicidal. This general is a friend of Hitler's, and there is no way he can let us live if we say no. It is as serious as that."

Mary Anne began to sob, and Mary consoled her.

"I am sorry to upset you with my frankness. However, we must all agree on this one," John said firmly.

Mary replied reluctantly, "If there is no other way, you have my agreement."

The twins were also in agreement, and after a long silence, John stated their intentions with one sentence. "So when the general calls to see us tomorrow, we will pretend to be enthusiastic about the film unconditionally."

Mary knew she had to compromise with the others. How could she not! Their lives could be at stake.

Chapter 8

Propaganda to Hitler's Nazi regime was of vital importance. Joseph Goebbels, the Reich's propaganda minister, was in complete control of radio broadcasts, newspapers, photography and film. With Hitler's blessing, Goebbels used the mass media to skilfully manipulate the German public.

Fascist ideology was promoted particularly well with the use of photography and film because of their wide audience and capacity to corrupt the truth. Leni Ribbentrop's films were masterpieces of propaganda.

Photographs and filmmaking would be fully exploited, particularly in Nazi-occupied countries, to falsely demonstrate to the world that it was not so bad to be annexed and be a part of the Reich and sharing the prosperity of a powerful fascist state.

However, the reality was different, and only few living under occupation could benefit; the majority would suffer from its brutality. The propaganda film, that was about to be made, would portray ordinary people of the British Empire enjoying everyday life under the Nazis, and would proliferate, around the world, the ideals of fascism and the Reich, so it was important and given top priority.

Annexation of the British Empire, with its magnitude and demography, was an enormous prize for Hitler and the Nazi regime. He wanted the whole world to witness his achievement, so the task of production and direction was to be undertaken by the most talented and the very best of Germany and would be made in full colour with 35 mm film.

Hitler had already made plans to invade Russia, and the timing of this propaganda film would be immaculate. His woeful belief was that it would help the Bolshevik people to resist less during a German occupation of that vast country. The film would have subtitles in many languages so as to have maximum effect, and production would commence immediately to meet the deadline at the end of May.

Over four million men would be deployed in the Russian invasion, and the planned commencement date was 22nd June 1941. It would be known as Barbarossa and would be Hitler's greatest prize and quell his hatred of communism.

Chapter 9

Mary had told her parents and sister about their involvement in the film and, unsurprisingly, they were upset; however, even without knowing the full implications, they gave Mary their full support.

While the family were waiting for the German car to collect them—they were not told where they were going—John was still thoughtful about whether they had made the right decision to cooperate. He could not think of himself as a collaborator, but as a pragmatic man who knew they would all be executed by the Gestapo for non-compliance; it was a question now of survival for the family.

He had not seen his resistance friends for a while and wondered if they were okay or had been arrested. The thought had occurred to him that they were being held somewhere as hostages should his family not agree to work with the Germans. Anyway, it was speculation, and they were probably lying low.

The vehicle arrived, and Heinz fetched the family to drive them to an unknown destination. John sat in the front, while Mary and the twins were in the rear of the car. A few neighbours had gathered outside to find out what was happening, and this made the family very uneasy as well as nervous. Since they did not know their destination, they were intrigued by their journey.

John asked Heinz, "Where are we going? We would like to know. Can you please tell us, Heinz?"

"We are heading west, Herr Groves, to meet Leni Ribbentrop, the film director and camerawoman. General Von Klaus will be there to meet us at the hotel where you will be staying. I have arranged everything for you, including clothes, so you do not need any luggage. I hope I have not been too presumptuous, Frau Groves."

Mary replied somewhat sarcastically, "I was not aware we were staying, Heinz. Anyway, I am sure you have chosen our outfits correctly."

The family was beginning to warm to the general's aide. He was polite and extremely helpful in trying to put them at ease.

It was an interesting journey, and they could see what had happened to the West End of London since the invasion. Large red swastika flags were on all important buildings, like the Houses of Parliament, and even their beloved Westminster Cathedral was covered. But the worst shock was seeing Buckingham Palace covered with the ugly flags as if to make a statement like, 'The Nazi party rules this country!'

So utterly humiliating, John pondered. It was though what one would expect to see in an occupied country. *France is in the same predicament,* John thought ruefully.

When they did finally arrive at their destination, it was at a really plush five-star hotel, and there were German soldiers everywhere, particularly SS units. General Ludwig Von Klaus greeted the family warmly and offered them champagne and said, "It is my privilege and honour to introduce you to Leni, our most prestigious film director." She was standing next to him.

Mary immediately thought of how beautiful and well-dressed Leni was. Leni was eager and looking forward to seeing the family and was not disappointed.

The general has chosen well, she thought. "I am so pleased to meet you all. Such lovely, photogenic subjects. You will all look beautiful in my film."

The general was very informal with the family and promised them all a wonderful lunch, and then after, Leni would talk to them about the film.

John and Mary were overwhelmed by the etiquette at lunch and the conversation. Leni explained to Mary, who was sitting next to her, "I have also been an actress and a dancer, as well as a film director." She laughed. "So I am well qualified to work with you and John."

Mary explained that she was only a nurse and had never acted before.

"But that is exactly how I want you to be, Mary—completely natural and sincere. My camera lens will do the rest. And don't worry, my dear, you will be simply wonderful."

John, on the other hand, was finding it difficult to have a normal, if not mundane, conversation with such a high-ranking general and an aristocrat. Working with these Nazi leaders and the surroundings of the hotel were intimidating for him.

"My colleague Joseph Goebbels wishes to meet you after the film is finished," concluded Leni.

After lunch, they retired to a large room where there was more champagne on an enormous table with a photographic slide machine and photographs of Leni's previous work.

"Leni, please proceed," the general prompted.

Leni started, "This will be Germany's biggest and most powerful and important film we have made so far. The first location will be the East End. We will film you at your home. Then we will have film sets at the Buckingham Palace, Houses of Parliament, Trafalgar Square, Whitehall and the British Museum. Also I should like to take a few scenes along the Thames and the Tower of London and, of course, that wonderful bridge." She continued, "The next locations will be Oxford and Cambridge. Our führer is particularly interested in Oxford. It is very exciting for you, yah?"

The general interjected and explained, "John, you do not need to worry about security for your family. I will have this completely under control, and my top officers will be at your disposal, including Heinz. I do not expect trouble, so it is just a precaution."

It had not crossed John's mind about needing security, but he thanked the general and said, "When do we start?"

Leni answered, "Tomorrow morning at 10 a.m. precisely, and I hope the English climate is kind to us, yah?"

The general then said, "Naturally, you will be staying here throughout the filming, and your house will be guarded at all times."

"What about my job as a nurse?" Mary asked nervously.

"You do not have to worry, Mary. We have arranged everything, including a temporary nurse to take over until you are ready to return to work. Leni and I know what is important to you, so all you have to do is make a wonderful film for us, please! If you need anything at all, you must ask Heinz or myself," the general said reassuringly.

"Mary Anne and James—will they be able to attend their work?" Mary asked.

"No, but we will explain to their employers about their absence. We wish you all to be together while the film is being made. Sorry," the general answered apologetically.

Leni then proceeded to show previous films that she had made, deliberately omitting one of her most famous as it might have appeared too propagandist to the family. The general had previously ordered Leni not to show this film, and she reluctantly had to agree.

Photographic slides were also shown of France, Holland and Belgium—which were under occupation—where local people lived harmoniously with the German soldiers. "I hope you have enjoyed this demonstration and that you can understand now what is required. Just be natural, yah?" concluded Leni. It was obvious to the family that Leni was the consummate professional dedicated to her projects. This made them slightly nervous.

The family retired to their sumptuous suite to change clothes and freshen up. Beautiful dresses were provided for Mary and dress suits for John. He joked and said to Mary, "When Heinz was taking measurements the other day, I thought it was for my coffin."

Mary did not enjoy the joke too much. The twins were also provided for and were almost beginning to enjoy the whole affair.

The family then joined the general and Leni for dinner. Leni looked stunning, wearing a beautiful, long satin evening dress in midnight blue. A full necklace studded with diamonds and pearls cascaded down to her ample cleavage as her dress was low-cut. Mary was impressed, but she looked equally beautiful and more modest with less jewellery and dressed in another long pink taffeta dress. Heinz had chosen well after all.

John was overwhelmed. He had never seen his wife looking so wonderful and wished he could provide her with expensive and exquisite dresses, with genuine jewellery instead of the cheap cosmetic pieces she often wore. He and James both looked good in the black-tie outfits provided by Heinz. Mary Ann showed she was a very attractive teenager too.

John then remarked to James, "Our ladies scrub up well." James agreed.

It was a magnificent meal and all the better as they had not eaten properly due to the rationing and food shortages. Now they were living and being treated like celebrities. After dinner, they were escorted by Heinz back to their suite. Passing the hotel bar, the loud singing of German military songs by a group of officers could be heard, suggesting that the whole hotel was occupied by the elite German officer corps.

The whole family welcomed the chance to have some time on their own and be back in their room to contemplate about their decision to make the film. It had been a hectic day, and all were pleased to have some rest, but they remained apprehensive about the next day's incredible events.

Chapter 10

The party met at 7 a.m. for breakfast, and it was a beautiful morning. Then they were driven to John and Mary's home. They arrived just before 10 a.m., and the film crew set up the cameras. Unfortunately, a crowd of local people had gathered, attracted to the scene, and some were jeering at the Germans. The family was embarrassed, and the general tried to put them at ease by saying, "Don't worry when the scene is shot. Leni will make cuts before completion so everybody will look happy." That was not what was worrying John. He was more concerned about future reprisals against his family.

The day's first programme of filming was started on schedule with typical German precision. John and Mary had noticed that many of the featured people were actually German soldiers dressed in ordinary clothes and made to look typically English, and that some extras were German women.

So it really is staged, Mary thought.

Leni took some still shots and then a moving film of the family inside their home. They were asked to be natural and smile. Then Leni ordered them not to look so nervous, and they promptly obeyed. The scenes were quite simple, with Mary making tea for John and the twins. After they sat on the sofa, listening to the wireless and talking, Leni continued to film. After the day's filming, they returned warily to the hotel. Leni wanted to be in the car with the family so she could discuss the next day's events.

The family was relieved to be away from their neighbours, and that the first stage was completed. It was a very uncomfortable experience for them, and the general, sitting in the car next to Mary, was sympathetic and expressed how difficult it must have been for them.

"You were all very brave to do what you did in front of your friends, and I sincerely apologise for putting you through this," he added.

On the way back, Mary asked the general if her family could join them tonight for dinner, and he wholeheartedly agreed. "Of course, Mary, it will be our pleasure. Will they wish to stay?" he asked.

"Yes, please," Mary replied.

"The general and Leni seemed so agreeable with us, John," Mary whispered.

"I am beginning to like them too, and it is worrying since they are enemies and we do not know how it will all end," said John rather anxiously.

John was enjoying the luxurious lifestyle, wining and dining each night, and Mary just delighted in the more mundane things, like having a hot bath without using a kettle every night, no washing or ironing after a hard day of nursing patients.

"Let's just enjoy for the moment and not think too much about the future," John said.

The general and Leni were having a quiet word too. "The führer has ordered me to return to Berlin after we have completed filming for a meeting, so I will not be able to attend the premiere of your film in London, Leni."

"Is it important?" Leni was curious and disappointed.

"All meetings with the führer are important," he replied. The general secretly knew that he was going to be ordered to command panzer divisions for an ill-advised, planned invasion of Russia in June, a prospect that he was not happy with, for he knew it could have parallels with Napoleon's invasion of Russia 130 years earlier. It was impossible; however, to refuse Hitler could be dangerous for his family.

Many generals had the same view—opening another front line in the east could prove to be Germany's downfall. They had several clandestine meetings together, and all were of the opinion that it was a war that could not be won. General Ludwig Graf Von Klaus was not a Nazi, and he hated the SS and the Gestapo, but, like John, he was being forced to do things against his principles to keep his family safe.

After dining at the hotel, John and the general went to the bar and continued drinking schnapps. The rest of the family had gone to bed, and as the evening went on, they were becoming quite drunk and speaking more openly.

For the first time, John was comfortable calling the general Ludwig, and he asked, "How did you win your Iron Cross?"

"I was awarded the medal in 1940 for a successful campaign during the Battle of France. The men under my command deserved it more! But the führer was pleased that the invasion I had helped to organise which was executed with military precision. For personal reasons, I asked Hitler not to involve me in the invasion of your country, and he agreed." Ludwig went on, slightly stuttering because of the effects of the schnapps, "At that time, I had respect and high regard for his genius and military acumen. However, strange decisions were being made, and the persecution of the Jews began to change my opinion."

"Do you have a family in Germany?" asked John.

"Yah, I have two sons and a beautiful daughter—all in their twenties. The sons are serving in the Wehrmacht and are both officers, and my daughter is a doctor. I am very proud of them."

"You and Heinz seem very close. Is he Gestapo?" asked John.

"He works with the Gestapo but is not one of them," replied Ludwig rather evasively, adding, "he is my man on the inside, as it were.

"My wonderful wife, Angelika, looks after our home, and I miss them all very much when I am away." Ludwig was slightly tearful, but it wasn't just the alcohol that made him melancholic. He was genuinely sad for his country, but he was careful not to say too much to John. "My father was one of the youngest Prussian generals. They were at that time all elderly men. He was a breath of fresh air. Father was in Marshall Foch's train carriage when Germany surrendered at the end of the last war," Ludwig proclaimed. "He was a proud man, my father, and after such a crushing defeat, he took his own life. The humiliation for him was too much. My dearest mother passed away soon after. Being the eldest son, I inherited his title and estates and have four siblings. Anyway, enough of me. I talk too much when I am drunk."

This man is definitely not a Nazi, John thought, and he began to talk about his own background. "Both my parents are dead too, and I have no brothers or sisters. They died because they lived in London. They both had consumption—TB, they call it now. I served my country at the Somme as a conscript. After being wounded, I was immediately evacuated back to England and remained scarred, as you can see. The pain was so severe that I wanted to take my own life as well. The shell shock started when I arrived at the hospital in Aldershot. It was awful. However, Mary, my nurse at the time, helped me through it all, and we married in 1918. Our children were born in 1922, and I love them both dearly. I would do anything to protect them. I have always been interested in military life and would have liked to have fought in this war, but my injuries and age, I suppose, stopped all my ambitions in that direction. What will happen to us after the filming, Ludwig? I fear for my family all the time," John asked.

"My friend, I have a fondness for your family and will do everything I can to help you all. We are living during difficult times, but I promise you will be safe while I am alive," Ludwig answered.

"Thank you. I trust you."

And then they both left to retire to bed as it was gone 1 a.m. John had seen the human side of Ludwig that night, and what he saw, he liked. *If only all Germans were like him, they would not be invading other countries and causing death and destruction,* he thought.

Buckingham Palace was the first film set the very next morning, and all were in position with cameras and lights. The palace looked empty and forlorn with a swastika flag flying at half mast, as if to incite the British nation. John asked if it could be taken down during filming. Leni consulted with the general, and he agreed to have it removed.

"It is an insult to our king and queen, and could cause a riot," John spoke boldly.

"Yah, I have no doubt it would, but we cannot allow a Union Jack, so we must reach a compromise, John. The area has been cordoned off, and the Londoners have not seen it, so no harm done. I must warn you that Joseph Goebbels may insist that we use the flag," the general said firmly.

"Thank you," said John.

Hitler had given strict orders that nobody must enter the palace—he wanted to save that honour for himself for his next visit to England—except for cleaning it must remain empty. The general knew this, however, and gave his word not to discuss or film inside, and that included Leni.

Leni was a master at organising people in front of the camera and seemed to know exactly where the most flattering light would be on each subject—no wonder she was chosen for this massive project. She was also taking many still shots as well, and Mary was posing mostly for these.

"Mary, you are so photogenic, darling. You have a typically English rose complexion that suits my camera lens. These pictures will look wonderful," Leni said, becoming very excited about seeing the processed and final result.

They had posed for still shots outside of the palace and were filmed by Leni with the extras in the grounds, but the general forbade them to go inside. The family and Leni were a little upset by this but accepted the decision. Ludwig had given his word.

John was still embarrassed in front of the camera and was always pleased when it was finished for the day. The twins, however, were just enjoying all the attention, and their natural demeanours seemed perfect for Leni's lens. John and Mary were asked to hold hands and walk in the gardens, stopping to admire the flower beds.

John remarked quietly to Mary, "It's all so false. I'm dreading having to sit through it all."

Filming at the Houses of Parliament was excellent since they were allowed to go inside for shots and moving pictures of the historic building. It was important as it meant so much to the British, and to show to the world that a fascist government was in control of one of the oldest democracies in the world was a major coup for Hitler and his Nazi regime.

Trafalgar Square was another important film set with Nelson's Column, one of the most important heroes of the British Empire history for his victory over the French at the Battle of Trafalgar. Hitler loved heroes, and the Third Reich was a legacy of the old Germanic knights. Hitler's orders, again, were to not enter the National Gallery under any circumstances as he alone wanted to visit first and see the famous paintings—some by

German artists. Looting by any German soldier by whatever rank would be punishable by death—this was the edict pronounced.

Whitehall was the last part of the filming schedule that day, and filming passed without incident. There were a few protesters but no arrests. Everybody was pleased to return to the hotel for dinner and a good night's rest after such a long day. The next morning, the British Museum was filmed but only outside as the security guarding all the valuable treasures might have been compromised. Even the general himself was not allowed to enter in case something went missing. The treasure and relics contained inside would most likely be sent to Germany in the future, as well as those in the National Gallery. After lunch, the Thames, including the Tower of London and Tower Bridge, finished the day's filming, and the exhausted party was eager to return to the hotel and then dinner.

With her boundless energy and enthusiasm, Leni had set a rigorous two days, but even she was tired, and all retired to their rooms early.

With the London filming completed, they went to Oxford and Cambridge for two days. Leni was particularly excited about filming in Oxford to impress Hitler as she knew he had special plans for the city in the future. Hitler had mentioned to the general many times during meetings at the Berghof that Oxford was a special place and must never be bombed.

The general's lack of interest in the film was beginning to be noticed by Leni, and his disdain of Hitler was becoming more and more difficult to hide. Leni had been aware of it for some time and asked him candidly why he lacked enthusiasm for the film he had helped to produce. "Leni, I have other things on my mind" was his restrained answer, for he knew how fervent Leni's loyalty was to her führer.

One day when the filming was finally coming to its end after much hard work, General Von Klaus did not appear on the film set, and John and Mary wanted to know why. Leni explained that it was no mystery. Ludwig had been ordered back to Berlin for another meeting with the führer. He would be returning soon with Joseph Goebbels.

"Please, I ask you not to worry as your family has done a wonderful job for the Reich and you will be famous," Leni said nervously. "We have met all our targets, and in a few days, the film will be processed and completed. I thank you all for your help. I am so proud to have worked with you." She continued, "I will miss your family so much."

Mary replied, "We will miss you and Ludwig as well."

Chapter 11

On 27th May 1941, the hotel was buzzing with excited Germans as the finished film was going to be shown to the general, Goebbels and many leading Nazis, including Himmler. Hitler would not be there as was originally thought as he had other 'pressing matters to attend to'.

This was in reference to the invasion of Russia. Leni was disappointed and expressed her annoyance to the general, who seemed to be unusually worried and in a pensive mood. They were both unhappy as well that Himmler would be there, since their dislike of Himmler and the SS had been simmering for years.

"I thought that the führer wished to see my film in England, the country he has conquered. Instead we have this parasite," Leni said scathingly to the general in reference to Himmler.

"Leni, I'm afraid the führer has told me that he will need to delay his personal viewing of the film and wishes to see it with our English stars in Berlin soon. Matters that cannot be discussed are deemed to be more important to him than another visit to London, and he sends his best wishes to you and for the premiere of the film."

That afternoon was the premiere of the long-awaited film, and John, Mary and the twins were presented to Goebbels and Himmler. A few words were spoken as everybody was eager for the film to start. All were slightly nervous by the presence of the two top Nazis, with the exception of the general, whose disdain for both men seemed noticeable. But he was one of the führer's favourites, so toleration and respect had to be reluctantly shown towards him. The atmosphere was tense for John. He hated the thought of being in the same room as Hitler's fascists leaders, but it was too perilous not to show respect for the top Nazis.

In the specially prepared auditorium at the hotel, about fifty people, all seated, were eagerly awaiting the start, but before commencing, Leni addressed the 'distinguished' audience. "It is a great honour for me to introduce my film to you and to welcome our most distinguished guests. The film was originally the brainchild of our führer and minister present here. Unfortunately, our führer is not with us today, but has sent a message to us all, expressing his wish that he is looking forward to seeing it in Berlin next week."

The audience then rose to their feet and saluted, "Heil Hitler!" John and Mary stood as well after being prompted by the general.

The film lasted for two hours with an interlude in between, and at the finish, the audience cheered and clapped for many minutes, showing their appreciation. It had been a great success, and Leni, the general and the family were all relieved and pleased for different reasons that it was now all over. All the Nazi audience wanted to meet the English family that had helped to make such a wonderful film. Any anxieties that they had gave way to euphoria, and they were for now enjoying the moment.

After dinner that same day, Ludwig was anxious to speak with John and Mary about his return to Berlin. "My dear friends, having spent so much time with you and becoming fond of you all, it is my duty to protect you and ensure your safety. I worry that you may not be safe here in England as you may be considered by your own people as collaborators with Germany, so my responsibilities towards you are not ending, and it is important to me that you are safe. I would like to suggest you stay with my wife in Germany for a while after we have had our meeting with Hitler.

"My ancestral home is a castle in Baden-Württemberg, not too far from Stuttgart, and is a wonderful and peaceful place. You can stay there for as long as you wish." The General continued, "There is another private matter that I should like to tell you, but I can only discuss this with you when we are alone. Please take time to think about my proposition as I know it is an important decision."

Initially, Ludwig's request came as a shock, but they were so pleased that he was showing concern for them. So they thought about his offer seriously; after all, who would not want to spend some time in a castle?

Now that they were alone, Ludwig needed to get something off his chest. "Hitler has ordered me to return to Berlin tomorrow, and I must ask you to come with me. The Luftwaffe has arranged for an aircraft to take us to Berlin tomorrow afternoon, as I have orders to command several army divisions for a military campaign. That's all I can tell you at the moment.

"I hope you decide to come with me back to my home and stay with my wife in Baden. Angelika gets very lonely in that big old castle and would love for you to stay with her." He laughed.

Mary was shaken as it was so sudden. "Ludwig, what about my parents?" she enquired anxiously.

"If they cannot be ready in time, we can arrange for them to follow. Heinz will arrange this for you. I trust Heinz with my life, so I know he will do whatever is necessary for us," replied Ludwig.

John intervened and said, "Mary, we have very little choice, and for the safety of the twins, we must go tomorrow with Ludwig. Heinz is loyal to Ludwig, and we can depend on him to arrange for your parents and Elizabeth to follow us." Mary was reluctant but agreed.

Ludwig was so pleased that they were coming with him as he felt responsible for the dangerous position they now faced. Besides that, he was extremely fond of his new English friends, and he wanted to protect them. John was bemused somewhat and wondered how this aristocratic German general would want to make friends with a working-class family living in the East End of London; however, he was pleased for the whole family that it was so, and knew he could depend on this charismatic man.

After a tearful departure from the hotel the next day and leaving Mary's parents behind, John, Mary and the twins boarded a Luftwaffe aircraft at Biggin Hill aerodrome. The general and Leni were on the same flight bound for Berlin, and the plan was that they would stay in Berlin for a few days at the behest of Hitler, and then Ludwig would take them to Baden via Stuttgart.

John and Mary had never flown before and were both very apprehensive. The twins saw the whole trip as an adventure and were relaxed and looking forward to the flight. James was interested to learn about the aircraft and asked the general, "Sir, what is this aircraft called? It is quite large."

The general was glad to answer and appreciated James's interest. "It is a Focke-Wulf FW200 transport aircraft, and is one of the safest and most reliable in the Luftwaffe. Hitler has a specially converted one when he travels by air."

"How many passengers does it carry?" asked James.

"This particular version seats twenty-six and has been in service since 1937. I have a wonderfully illustrated book of many German aircrafts that you can read when we are at my home, James. I also have a keen interest in aircrafts," the general replied.

"Thank you, sir. I will look forward to reading it," James answered politely.

John was listening to the conversation and was very impressed and pleased that James was interested in the military just as he had been at eighteen. *A chip off the old block,* he thought.

A few hours later, they were in Berlin and checking into a hotel close to the chancery. Ludwig knew that they would be summoned by Hitler very soon. Goebbels and Himmler were on an earlier flight with other high-ranking Nazis, and they were already in Berlin.

Ludwig was hoping that he would have a meeting with Leni, Goebbels and Hitler at the same time. His distrust of Goebbels was intense, and they hardly agreed on any matters concerning state affairs. The general was influential within the Wehrmacht high command, and he knew Hitler's reliance on and support from the army was of paramount importance for his invasion of the Soviet Union.

The political party of the Reich mostly resented the army and its generals, but respect was reluctantly always shown to Hitler's favourites, such as Ludwig.

They gathered in the hotel bar a few hours later, and Ludwig was quick to mention that the family would be called upon to see Hitler at a moment's notice, and that they should be prepared for this. "When it happens, Leni will be with us to show Hitler the film and explain everything to him, so please do not worry as I will be with you at all times. I know how difficult it will be confronting the main man responsible for invading your country. Hitler will only speak to you in German. His English is limited to a few words, and I will translate for you."

Leni now joined them at the bar, saying, "We must all be relieved now that the film is over. I am very proud of this wonderful family. I consider this as my finest work, and I know the führer will honour you."

She knew Hitler very well and, some would say, was able to manipulate him to some extent, but he was often moody and unpredictable, so she was always careful not to upset him. Leni was confident that he would like the film and the English family, and would view it as a major propaganda victory.

Some years ago, Leni, as an aspiring young actress, craved to have an affair with Ludwig. She was unmarried, and her private life was unfulfilled. Ludwig—a wealthy, dashing, charismatic and powerful man—had all the qualities that attracted her. But he was already happily married and rejected her advances; thereafter, an uneasy friendship remained between them.

They continued to work together on many projects, and both had a great deal of respect for each other in spite of Leni being more pro-Nazi than he; however, Hitler liked them both, and they were both considered as favourites and part of his inner circle, often visiting the Berghof, Hitler's retreat in Bavaria.

Chapter 12

Hitler had summoned the general, Leni, Goebbels and the family for a preview of the film before it would be, "released to the world," as he proclaimed. The general introduced John, Mary and the twins to him, and Hitler showed some warmth in his greeting. Because of the English civilians, no "Heil Hitler" salutes were given.

He went to the twins first and, putting both hands on their cheeks, said in German, "Meine Kinder Sie sind nun teil des Reiches, und wir ehren." (My children, you are now part of the Reich, and we honour you.) The twins were overwhelmed and confused but remained calm. They were both eighteen years old, but he still referred to them as children.

Hitler then turned to John and Mary. "Die Volker des Reiches ich danke ihnen fur ihren Beitrag zu unserer wundervollen Film. Wir werden nun genielben sie Zusammmen." (The people of the Reich thank you for your contribution to our wonderful film. We will now enjoy it together.)

The general translated for them, and Leni proceeded to show the film, Hitler and Goebbels sat in between the twins and John and Mary. The general was behind them both to translate if any questions were asked by the führer.

After the film finished, Hitler clapped enthusiastically and smiled. Then he said one simple word in English, "Wonderful!"

The ordeal for the family was over. Nothing more could have been so terrible for the family than for John and Mary to watch this evil man touch their family, and then to shake hands with the man responsible for invading their country. It was an experience that they had to endure to save their lives, and for a while after, they could not stop shaking. To resist meant arrest by the Gestapo. It was such a relief for all, including Ludwig, that it was all over and that they would soon be in the serenity and peace of the castle.

Ludwig was anxious to see his wife, and he took the family to Baden by taking the short flight to Stuttgart from Berlin, and then a road journey to his home situated in the beautiful Black Forest district. It was an area of outstanding natural beauty during any season, and the family was seeing it in summer. With the wild flowers adorning the mountains wherever one looked and the evergreen pines tall and ancient with an extravaganza of shades of green, this gave the family a feeling of well-being, and they were so happy to be away from London.

The general's chauffeur was waiting for them with a big smile. He had missed his count very much. Ludwig had been away for three months, so it was such a relief to reach the gates of the castle.

"Welcome home, Count," said the chauffeur as they arrived. Nobody referred to him as the general in these parts. He was known only as the count, a title he preferred. He was always happy to forget the Nazi nonsense, as he called it.

On their arrival at the castle, two large solid wooden doors were opened, and they were greeted by Angelika, who welcomed them all with hugs and kisses on both cheeks. She said, "It is such a pleasure to meet my husband's friends. I have looked forward to it so much, and I hope you will give me the honour of becoming my friends."

Mary was so thrilled with such a genuinely warm welcome that she shed a tear and said, "You are so kind to us, Countess, in allowing my family to stay in your beautiful home."

"You are most welcome, Mary, and please feel free to do whatever you wish." She looked at the twins and pronounced, "There is so much for you to explore here at the castle and many sporting activities. John, you must need a beer. Mary, please call me Angel. Only the servants address me as Countess, so kindly enter our home as they are all excited and waiting to meet you." Angelika then turned to her husband, and they both embraced.

The servants were all lined up and were introduced formally. There were six men—including a butler, a coachman and a driver (whom the family had already met)—and the other men were for garden maintenance, headed by Victor. All bowed and shook hands. The ladies consisted of a housekeeper, cook, maids and

Angelika's personal maid, and each curtsied; even the twins were shown this charming courtesy. John and Mary were being treated like royalty, and the castle and its grounds were so beautiful and grand.

"Shall we dine at 6 p.m. after you have rested?" asked Angelika, and then she looked at the chef to confirm.

John and Mary and the twins were shown to their respective rooms. Mary Anne was excited to see her room and was not disappointed; it had a large balcony overlooking the forest. Pine trees sloping down into a valley made the scene so dramatic. There was a large double bed and beautiful velvet curtains.

The maid asked in her limited English, "If you need anything, please pull this, Fräulein Mary Anne." She showed Mary Anne the bell chord.

Mary Anne was embarrassed because she was not used to being waited on, but the experience was like a fairy tale, she thought. She replied to the maid, "Thank you."

James's room was the same and was next door, and he could not wait for the maid to leave so he could explore his surroundings.

John and Mary were eagerly awaiting to see what their room would be like, and when the maid opened the door, they could not believe how magnificent it was. The first thing they noticed was the four-poster bed and the large French doors leading to the balcony with views so stunning it took their breath away.

"Do you like your room, Madam Frau?" the maid asked.

"Yes, it is wonderful. Thank you," Mary replied.

"Please ring my bell chord if you need anything, Madam Frau." And then she left the room.

"I can imagine the rooms in Buckingham Palace are like this, Mary," said John.

"The whole castle is so beautiful, and Angelika is too. It is like a wonderful dream that we are here, and I keep thinking that I will wake up, and it will abruptly end," remarked Mary.

"Just enjoy it while we can, Mary, as someday we will have to go back to England. I don't think I'm going to miss London too much," John chuckled.

When the family went downstairs to the dining room, Mary was quick to thank Angelika again for allowing her family to be her guests at the castle, and she explained modestly that they had never experienced anything so grand and beautiful. Angelika replied, saying, "It is Luds (her nickname for her husband) and my privilege to have you stay here, and we hope you can relax and recover from your experiences over the last six months. The invasion of your country by the Nazis must have been horrible for your family, Mary, and Luds has told me that your parents and sister will be safely with us very soon. He has arranged for a flight, and Heinz will be with them throughout the journey. You do not have to worry about anything, Mary, while you are here."

Angel continued with her enthusiasm to have the family with her in her home. "Tomorrow we can go to Stuttgart for shopping for clothes for you all. There isn't very much in Baden that's very fashionable, unfortunately."

"We have no money here, Angel!" Mary explained.

"Oh, but you do, Mary. Hitler has authorised a large payment for you to show his and Germany's appreciation for working on the film. You are rich and can buy whatever you want."

"I don't know what to say," Mary replied.

Mary Anne then spoke to Angelika, "Countess, you are so beautiful and wear such lovely dresses."

"Thank you, Mary Anne. I am like a butterfly. Take away the wings, and I am not so good," she joked.

At that moment, Ludwig appeared, apologising profusely for keeping his guests waiting, and then they proceeded to the dining room. "My friends, earlier I went to the bank in Baden to collect the money for you. That is why I was late. It is a large sum, and I suggest you keep it in your room as there is a safe behind one of the paintings of an ancestor of mine. I do not trust our banks at this moment, so please keep it here," Ludwig reassured them.

"Ludwig, how can we ever repay you? You have kept every promise, and your and Angel's hospitality to my family has been amazing," John said honestly to both Ludwig and Angelika. "Thank you."

Angel then replied. "You are our friends, and we are grateful and value every moment you can stay with us. You will meet my daughter in Stuttgart tomorrow, and we can all have lunch. She is a doctor and works at the hospital. Unfortunately, my two sons are away somewhere, and it's a secret! How can you keep a secret like that from a mother, Luds?" she said jokingly.

"I should like to give you all a tour of the castle and the estate before we dine, if you are not too tired," said Ludwig. He was excited and wanted to convince his guests how much they would enjoy their stay.

"We would love to," replied John.

There were many stairs to climb, and Mary knew it would be tiring, but she was also excited to see the beautiful gardens.

"This room is where I was born fifty-four years ago," announced Ludwig. It was simple and unpretentious, not at all like the other bedrooms, but it had a special place in Ludwig's family history. "All the Von Klaus babies were born in this room for generations," he said proudly.

"I was Mama's firstborn on 17th November 1887. The name I bear is the same as my father's. I am glad that he is not alive to witness the terrible events of this war. He would have been ashamed of Germany and its association with the Nazi Party and treatment of the Jews. He deplored anti-Semitism and persecution of any race or religion. Father was opposed to the First World War and its militaristic demands on other nations even though his position as a high-ranking general was profoundly compromised."

"Were you involved in the last war? You never mentioned it, Ludwig," John asked.

"Yes, I wanted to fight at the front, but Father used his influence, and I was assigned to the general high command office as *Offizier im Gerneralstab*—sorry, that is a general staff officer. He and Mama did not want me to be at the front, and I resented it for a while. My apologies to you, Mary. I am becoming a bore."

"So you are, Luds. Continue the tour please!" remarked Angelika impatiently.

Going down the long galleried staircase to the ground floor, they entered a room about thirty metres in length. A beautiful, rich red carpet reached from one end to the other, and on each wall were portrait paintings.

"This is my favourite room," said Ludwig. "Here are the paintings of my ancestors, and this one is of my father and mother. It was painted soon after their wedding in 1885."

"Oh, she was so beautiful, Ludwig," said Mary.

"Yes, she was," replied Ludwig tearfully.

As they moved along the gallery, Ludwig pointed to another painting of his grandfather dressed in full Prussian uniform adorned with an Iron Cross. "This Von Klaus was probably the most illustrious and famous of all my ancestors and was a personal friend of the King of Prussia who later became emperor of Germany, or Kaiser. His daughter was the grand duchess of Baden, with whom my mother became quite friendly. She visited the castle on many occasions, and I saw the duchess several times as a young boy, I recall."

They moved on. An impressively large painting of Ludwig's father in full military uniform was proudly displayed. "This is my father, also called Ludwig. He was a full-blooded Prussian general with high principles, an honourable man, fiercely protective of his family and his country. He was also a disciplined authoritarian when it came to his sons, ensuring we upheld the good name of the Von Klaus," Ludwig concluded tearfully and apologised for being emotional. Angel then prompted everyone to move on.

The twins were fascinated by the many spiralling staircases that led to mysterious rooms. James thought that they might have been used to imprison captured soldiers in olden times, and Mary Anne said, "Maybe they were for locking away badly behaved brothers."

That caused everybody to laugh, and Mary joked, "Yes, so be good, or you might find yourselves locked in one."

After the full tour of the castle, they went outside into the gardens, and Angel took over. "This is my favourite place." She spoke to Victor, the head gardener, and Mary was quick to state that she had never seen such a beautiful garden. The elderly gardener thanked her profusely, and Angel praised him and explained, "We are very lucky to have Victor. He has transformed the gardens into something really special, and was here with Luds's father. Many of the taller trees and shrubs were planted by Ludwig's great-grandfather. During every season, it looks so different, so one never tires of its natural beauty. During the austerity period just after the first war, Ludwig's father was forced to make decisions about the upkeep of the gardens, and Victor was just amazing, managing to keep everything in good order with less planting."

Mary was immensely impressed and just loved the tranquillity of it all, with the fountains and the exquisite layout of the beautiful flowers with their exuberant colours. "Angel, I could live here for the rest of my life," she said appreciatively.

"Thank you, Mary and John, I hope you enjoyed the tour, and now if Luds, bless him, is satisfied that he has shown you everything, we will go back to the dining room. You must be quite hungry now." Angel beckoned everybody.

As they sat down to dine, John and Mary were still in a euphoric state and thinking how lucky they were to be here in this wonderful place; it was perfect.

During the meal, Mary commented about Angel's eloquence in English.

"That's because I am half English. Luds, did you not tell John and Mary! My father was the German ambassador to Britain in the late 1800s and met my English mother during one of his visits there. She was working as a secretary to the British ambassador. They were married in Berlin, and I am their first child. Luds, I am surprised you did not mention this to our friends. Ah, men! All they think and talk about are politics and wars," Angelika commented sarcastically.

"Oh, that's wonderful, Angel. It must be one of the reasons we get on so well," said Mary.

After the superb meal, the ladies along with the twins went into the drawing room, while John and Ludwig remained and were alone. "John, I have something to tell you, and it must remain within these walls. It is top secret, but I feel you must know. Germany is going to launch an invasion of Russia, and regretfully, Hitler has ordered me to command an army group with many panzer divisions. It will commence on 22nd June, in three weeks' time. I am regretful because I believe it is a war we cannot win and is dangerous for my country. You probably know by now that I am not a Nazi and detest the whole fascist ideology. Just wearing my uniform offends me, and I wish I was not part of this unnecessary and tragic war."

"Thank you for the trust you have in me, Ludwig. I am shocked and upset that you will have to leave your family and your home again so soon, but does Angelika know yet?" John asked.

"No, I am waiting for the right moment," replied Ludwig. He went on to say, "Your family will be safe here, and Hitler assumes it will be all over before the end of the winter," Ludwig explained very sarcastically.

"Ludwig, if there is anything Mary and I can do while you are away, please let me know."

"Thank you, John. Please take care of Angel and my daughter for me. I'm not sure when I will be back, and it will be a great comfort for me to know you and Mary are here with her. She puts on a brave face, I know, but she worries about me and the difficulties I have working with the Nazis. I am a soldier, not a politician, I keep telling myself."

John then said frankly, "I have the same problem, Ludwig. My conscience is one of guilt and deep concern that I have betrayed my country by cooperating and taking blood money from a country that has invaded my own. I cannot face looking in the mirror these days as I see a traitor."

"John, you must not see it this way. You were compelled by events to protect your family, and I have done the same," replied Ludwig. "I have known about your connection with a resistance movement, and it was the reason you were chosen to help with the film initially. But as time went by, my priority was to protect you and your family from the Gestapo as well. This is why I wanted you here.

"Heinz has left England and will be arriving with Mary's parents and sister this very evening, and they should be here at the castle before 10 p.m. I did not mention this to Mary in case the flight is delayed."

John had suspected that Ludwig knew of his partisan activities and was not shocked or surprised by the admission by Ludwig, but he asked him earnestly about his comrades, "What has happened to my friends?"

"The information I have is that they are still being held by the Gestapo. Heinz will give us some more details tonight when we see him." Ludwig then responded by saying, "John, I hope you have no hard feelings about this. I am your friend and will be always loyal to you."

"No, Ludwig, I am truly grateful to you for saving my family, and knowing you have taken many risks to do this, we owe you a great deal." And then two men hugged each other and went to join the ladies.

Chapter 13

At about 10 p.m. that evening, Heinz arrived with Mary's parents and sister to the relief of everyone, including the servants. There was such a tearful reunion and joy that they were all together once more and safe in the home of the Von Klaus's. Tired from their exhaustive journey, Mary's family retired to their rooms.

Mary was so grateful to Ludwig that she went to him and said, "I will remember what you have done for my family for the rest of my life. Thank you." And she kissed him on both cheeks.

Heinz was very informative regarding John's friends and said that they were still alive, and that the Gestapo had not arrested their families. "Heinz and I will do everything we can to save them, John. Heinz has much influence within the Gestapo. However, he hates them and the SS as much as we do and blames them for his own parents' death, isn't that so, Heinz?"

"Yah, Herr General."

And with that, they all retired to their rooms.

After breakfast the next morning, everybody boarded two cars to take them to Stuttgart. Ludwig, surprisingly, wanted to take the wheel, complaining that he had not driven for three months. It was a lovely sunny day, and the sky was clear. The good weather gave the family a chance to enjoy the picturesque landscape of the Black Forest as they drove towards the city, and all were in good spirits.

Ludwig wanted to let his friends know how much he always missed the beautiful and stunning scenery of his beloved Schwartzwald (Black Forest). "Whenever I am away from home, I think of this beautiful area, and I become sad. I love this place so much. My family has lived here for generations and can be traced back 600 years, you know," said a nostalgic Ludwig.

"Angel, you must take our friends to one of the cuckoo clock factories. They have been making these wonderful clocks for 300 years. And let them visit the Feldberg, the highest mountain in Germany outside of the Alps."

"Oh, Luds, they have only just arrived here. I must apologise for his impatience for you to see everything, my friends," said Angel.

"No, don't apologise, Angel. Ludwig's love for his country is so admirable, and we love it too," replied Mary.

Today the war seems a million miles away, but later today, I will tell my beloved wife about me going to Russia, Ludwig promised himself, determined not to spoil Angelika's special day. She was with good friends and was seeing her daughter, and that always made her happy.

When they arrived at the hospital where Heidi worked, she was eagerly waiting, and she kissed everybody with a warm greeting. She was an attractive blonde young woman with blue eyes, wearing a smart suit and matching hat, and she spoke very good English. "It is such a pleasure to meet you all. Mary Anne, you are so pretty! We will find some stylish clothing shop for you too. Lunch first, and then we will go shopping, ladies." She took hold of Mary's and her mother's arm. "Mama has told me you are a nurse, Mary, and we are both in the same profession."

"Yes, Heidi."

"After, the men can go to a bar, and John will discover what his friend, my father, is really like," she said jokingly.

Lunch was a typical Bavarian meal with plenty of poultry, sauerkraut and good white wine. Even during wartime, there still seemed to be plenty of food here unlike Britain, where rationing of all foods had been instigated and enforced by the Nazis.

But how long will it last after Germany invades Russia? Ludwig thought.

Mary knew the kind of clothes that John and her son liked, so she would shop for them, and for the first time in their lives, they did not have to worry about money. She had Reichsmarks and plenty of them! The men then went to a Bierkeller, while the ladies shopped, and the alcohol flowed freely with litre jugs of good-quality Bavarian beer.

When it comes to drinking beer, these Germans are real professionals, and I am out of my league, thought John. Ludwig and Heinz were way up on John and James. "You and Heinz will not be able to drive back, you know," said John, feeling very merry.

"No problem. My chauffer and butler are coming in another car to drive us all back."

John, in spite of his intoxication, was relieved to know this. John and Ludwig had had so many drinking days together now, and it always ended up with both men being drunk, but today Ludwig would need the Dutch courage to help him tell Angel about his orders from Hitler, a task he did not relish.

When they all arrived safely back at the castle—including Heidi—Ludwig asked Angelika and Heidi to accompany him to the drawing room and immediately began to explain about his orders to go to Russia; however, he avoided giving too much information to them. "You know I love you both and miss you each time I go away. It is with sadness that I must tell you that Hitler has ordered me to go to Russia and I must leave tomorrow." Mother and daughter were distressed by the bad news as it seemed he had only just come back from England.

What a sad way to end such a lovely day, thought Heidi. "Do you know how long you will be away, Papa?"

"Unfortunately not, but it looks likely till the end of the year at least."

Angel tried desperately to hold back her tears, trying not to upset Ludwig and her daughter.

Ludwig then explained that he was very pleased that the Groves family was staying at their home while he was away, mainly to lighten the mood somewhat. "I will ask the driver to take us to Stuttgart tomorrow morning, and we can say our goodbyes there."

Dinner that evening was a very sombre occasion, but with everyone there, including Heinz, Ludwig tried his best to help raise everybody's spirits; however, he was reasonably certain that his return to Germany would not be by the end of the year. His grave concern was that the Wehrmacht would be bogged down by the weather after initial success. This would give the Soviet Army time to regroup and counterattack. His military experience was vast, and he, unlike Hitler, knew the pitfalls of a war against an adversary such as Russia with seemingly endless resources of manpower and armaments.

Poland and the Baltic States were quickly conquered, and Britain and France fell relatively easily, but to have a long-term Eastern front was suicidal. Hitler was making decisions as the supreme commander that would inevitably lead to a disaster for Germany.

During dinner, Ludwig spoke to Mary's father, explaining to him that they were pleased that he, Mary's mother and Elizabeth were able to stay with them. He joked, "It is ironic that we had to bring you to Germany to escape from the Germans."

Peter laughed and replied, "It is nice here, and we feel safe, but how long should we stay?"

"Until it is safe to go back. That might be a very long time, but, eventually, both your families will return, so meanwhile, please feel at home," Ludwig replied sympathetically.

Mary was interested to know about the film and asked Ludwig.

"Mary, it is as we speak being shown in cinemas around all the occupied countries, and maybe others. So you are famous, particularly in Germany, and when you next go to Baden with Angelika and Heidi, you may be recognised, and people will ask for your autograph."

"Oh no! I would be embarrassed," she replied.

After dinner, the ladies, James and Mary's father went to the drawing room, and John and Heinz stayed back at Ludwig's request. He was anxious to speak with them. "John, before the end of the week, Heinz and I will be on the Poland–Russia border, creating an Eastern front line as Hitler planned. There is, however, another matter as dangerous as the Russian front. Heinz and I have been approached by the German Resistance Movement, a high-level organisation within the Wehrmacht, to join them, and this we are considering. You know I have been unhappy about the way Nazism is damaging my country, and Hitler's leadership will inevitably become unstable.

"Heinz and I cannot be true to our consciences and principles and remain as we are, because the movement is within the Wehrmacht. There are many high-ranking German officers like myself as well as politicians that are making plans to topple the present Nazi regime by assassinating Hitler. We have resisted this for now, but in the future, we may join them, and this will inevitably jeopardise our family's safety.

"Angelika and I own a chateau in Switzerland, and you must go there to save your family and mine, should they be in danger. You will be safe there as it is a neutral country. The Gestapo and the SS are cruel and vindictive and will seek revenge and come here should anything happen to Hitler in the future. I think we are looking at the long term as he is too popular and strong now. However, if the Russian campaign begins to falter, the movement will act. And if Heinz and I are implicated in a plot of some kind, we will both be executed. Please forgive me for being so blunt."

John was quick to reply, stating, "I will do whatever is necessary to protect your family, and I am in the same position as you are, so don't worry. You have my word."

Ludwig then asked John if he could make sure that his servants were protected as much as possible. "Some of them were with my mother and father and are so loyal to us, they will help you should you need to escape from the castle. There are two cars and a good supply of fuel for all of you to escape to Switzerland with provision for currency other than Reichsmarks, so we are prepared. Thank you, John. I can go to Russia now without this burden." They then joined the others for drinks.

Chapter 14

The next morning was very sad, as they said goodbye to Ludwig at the castle forecourt. Angelika, Heidi and Heinz left with him to go to Stuttgart, where he and Heinz would take a flight to Berlin and then take up his command of the massive campaign of Barbarossa.

Heidi would go to the her place of work at the hospital, and Angelika would return to the castle to join her guests. She felt that a strong bond had been developed with them all, particularly with Mary, and she was so happy that the family was staying with her while her husband was absent.

When Angelika returned, she was visibly upset, and Mary and John comforted her. John noticed that it was the only time Angel looked her age. She was in her fifties but always appeared to be a forty-year-old. *It is understandable,* he thought. To John, Mary said quietly of her, "She is an amazing, resilient person and will cope."

Life at the castle seemed to be getting back to normal after a few weeks, and John, Mary and the twins were enjoying the luxury of the estate with its stunning views and magnificent rooms. Being waited on was something that could not quite be normal for them, particularly Mary, who felt she should be helping the servants; however, they would respectfully not allow her to do anything other than make tea in their room.

Mary's parents and sister were also having a good and relaxing time. Mary's mother felt safe and secure at the castle, and that was enough for her to be happy. It was wonderful that they could all enjoy the lovely walks together. Ludwig's dogs were two male German shepherds named Axel and Kiefer. They were so much alike it was difficult to tell the difference. Peter gave up eventually. Angel's own dog was called Syd, and it was a cute cocker spaniel with very sad eyes. It followed Angel everywhere, but it took to Liz, and she was able to take him for a walk, which she adored.

The twins were learning how to ride their favourite horses and enjoyed the grooming. They helped to muck out the stables, where four horses were kept, and they became very friendly with the groom, who taught them so much of equine management. It was an idyllic existence, but how long would it last, was the general view. The family were shielded from the reality of the war and the hardships suffered by the English population. Naturally, feelings of guilt occurred almost daily, but survival was always paramount in all their minds.

As the time passed, the family reconciled with their situation, and travelling around the Black Forest became more frequent. Angel's chauffer was always at their disposal, willing to take them to different towns and villages.

On one occasion, Angel suggested they take the two cars into Stuttgart so the whole family and Angel could visit her daughter for lunch, and all were eager to go. As they were walking around the town, two strangers approached Mary and John—they were both men—and said, "You are the English family that made the film, yah? We enjoyed it so much. Are English people so happy to be part of Germany?"

John tried very hard not to be upset by the remarks and answered carefully, fearing that they may be Gestapo. He remembered Ludwig's advice that they were everywhere in Germany, and were mostly in plain clothes. "Yes, we are happy."

They then asked for their autographs. Mary declined to give them her signature and moved away, muttering to herself that they had lost everything, possibly their home, job, friends and self-respect.

Angel and Heidi were compassionate towards her, and Angel said, "Please try not to be upset, Mary. It was a foolish remark they made. We know that nobody could be happy having gone through the terrible trauma your family has suffered, and one day we will all help you to get back to your normal life—I promise."

"Thank you. You have been always so kind to us, and we are very grateful, but I do miss England so much," Mary replied, holding back her tears.

They then went to a good restaurant to have lunch, but Angel and Heidi had noticed that many of the shops and restaurants did not have a wide choice any more as was the case at the beginning of the war. It was apparent that even Germany was beginning to suffer shortages. *So what must it be like in the occupied countries?* thought Angel.

John was still pondering the incident and was deeply disturbed; it had awakened a great concern for him that the family would never be able to return to England again as they would always be considered as collaborators with Germany and traitors to England, and even if England would be freed from Nazi occupation, they might never be safe.

Chapter 15

The build-up of German troops and heavy armour, including Ludwig's panzer divisions, began to amass on the Soviet frontier, and Ludwig's commanders, with the largest concentration of tanks in history, were preparing to advance into Russia.

Ludwig had thoughts of his family back in Baden but tried hard to dismiss these as the moment had arrived for him to command thousands of German soldiers of the Wehrmacht. He was troubled, however, and found it difficult to reconcile his duty as a German officer with his loyalty to Hitler, and was now beginning to waver.

All of Ludwig's early ambitions and desires for a so-called idealistic Greater German Reich seemed to be diminishing into an abyss of brutality and desperation for his beloved Germany. The humiliations of the past, the defeat of Germany in 1918 and his father's suicide remained the worst tragedies in his life, and he could neither forgive nor forget. Germany, however, appeared to be heading inexorably towards another defeat.

The earlier success of the Nationalist Party, made possible by Hitler's charisma in the early thirties, greatly impressed Ludwig, but now he was seeing the dark side of a monster, with mass murders of civilians and tyrannical behaviour—this was intolerable for Ludwig.

For now though, he would use his prowess and leadership skills to guide his units to victory for the sake of his men and country.

The invasion of the Soviet Union began as scheduled on 22nd June 1941, and the Wehrmacht made incredible progress due to its blitzkrieg tactics. Ludwig's panzers spearheaded the attack with remarkable success, and the Soviet forces found themselves being routed. Hitler was delighted and sent a message to his favourite general, praising him for his bravery and promoting him to a field marshal.

"I'm not sure I want this now," proclaimed Ludwig to Heinz privately.

"It may help us in the future," replied Heinz.

Back in Baden, Hitler had sent a personal message to Angelika, informing her of her husband's success and promotion. It came as a complete surprise since she did not know anything about Ludwig's involvement; moreover, the invasion had been a secret. However, she was so pleased that he was well; letters were taking a lifetime to arrive from the front.

Angelika immediately told everybody and asked the driver to take her to Stuttgart so she could personally give Heidi the good news. She was still slightly worried about her sons and had not heard anything for months. The truth was that they were serving in Russia—but not in the same unit as Ludwig—and were well as far as it was known.

John was getting restless at not doing very much and wanted to know how things were in England. Had the resistance against the Nazis grown, and had they been successful? He thought that maybe Germany's military manpower was being stretched as a result of their war with the Russians, and that they were withdrawing soldiers from England.

As the months passed, it became increasingly obvious that the German forces were being gradually repulsed and that the Russians were beginning to win battles.

"They seem to have an endless supply of manpower," Ludwig said in one of his reports to Hitler. Hitler was furious and insisted Ludwig return for a meeting at the Wolf's Lair along with other leading generals of the high command.

At the meeting, Hitler announced that, as supreme commander, he was being forced to issue a direct order that no mechanised or infantry units must withdraw after it was admitted by one senior general that his divisions were under the threat of encirclement.

Hitler flew into a rage and accused the high command of cowardice, proclaiming, "You will fight to the death. There must never be any surrender of captured territory."

It would prove to be the catalyst for Ludwig to decide he would now join the German Resistance Movement as he knew

Hitler was demented and completely out of control and Germany was in great danger.

"Heinz, when we return to Germany, I will help to organise the assassination of Hitler with the German Resistance Movement before it is too late," proclaimed Ludwig.

The generals of the high command returned to their units on the Eastern Front, and some, including Ludwig, began making plans for the assassination of the führer. Hitler seemed to have a guardian angel when it came to attempts on his life. Several had been made before, but Hitler always escaped death. Now he had more enemies, so there was now a better chance to succeed.

Many high-ranking generals were of the opinion that Germany should sue for peace before it was too late, but none would speak out for fear of execution as traitors.

In Russia, the German Army was beginning to falter even further, just as Ludwig had feared. First, the rains came to impede movements of mechanised vehicles and tanks, and then the cold Russian winter brought the mobility of virtually everything to a standstill. Even the weapons were frozen and unable to fire. The snows had come, bringing misery to the German Army, and many soldiers were starving and frostbitten, unable to be an effective fighting force.

Hitler had assumed that the Russian forces would be defeated by summer, but the Wehrmacht cold-weather clothes and equipment were woefully inadequate for a Russian winter. This was the beginning of a terrible mistake, and Ludwig's predictions were proving to be accurate. It was going to be a long and costly winter for the Germans during 1942.

Ludwig, worried and concerned for the safety of his sons and using his influence and power as a field marshal, arranged for them to be transferred to his staff and promoted in rank so that he could keep them under his wing. He could not wait to inform Angelika and Heidi the good news that they were safe.

When the news arrived about her two sons, Angel was ecstatic, and immediately asked the driver to take her to Stuttgart so she could tell Heidi in person. She took Mary along with her.

"Heidi, wonderful news! Your father has been able to transfer your brothers to his own unit and will be able to keep an eye on them." Angel was so excited to give the good news to

Heidi as none of the family had heard anything about their whereabouts.

Heidi was so pleased that she cried for a while and said, "Mama, someday we will all be together again." And they gave each other a hug, and then turned to Mary to reciprocate.

The war for the German people had suddenly changed, and many now spoke privately of a possible defeat. All the hysteria and mystique surrounding the dictator was diminishing rapidly, and Britain was to be given a lifeline, albeit under tragic and treacherous circumstances.

Chapter 16

On 7th December 1941, the Japanese attacked Pearl Harbour in Hawaii, and finally, the Americans entered the war. When the news broke eventually, everybody suffering under the yoke of fascism in the occupied countries was given hope for the future that the Germans would lose the war and their countries would be liberated.

Top-secret plans were being made to land American forces, with their allies, on the shores of Britain for liberation, while the British government and the royal family, who were in exile in America, drew up plans to re-establish a government. The Allied countries would then launch a massive landing force to liberate the French and then the other occupied countries, with a final thrust towards Berlin.

These plans of liberation would take many months, even years, to develop into reality, for first the Japanese had to be repulsed from the Pacific.

When the two families learnt of the news that America had entered the war, they had mixed feelings and wondered how an invasion of Germany would affect them all. They were full of expectation that it would lead eventually to the eradication of Nazism throughout Europe, which was so detested by the Klaus and Groves families. But how would they be treated by the Allies?

Angelika and her family, although not Nazis, were still Germans, and as such would be considered as enemies by the Allies, since Ludwig and her two sons were officers of the Wehrmacht. The Groves family were worried also that they would be treated as traitors because of the film.

"It's too early to start worrying about that. There is still a lot to do to defeat Hitler and the Nazi regime, so any invasion to liberate could be many years away," said John.

"You're right, John," Angel said, "Let us just enjoy this moment and celebrate with champagne, that Ludwig and my sons are okay. Gather the servants, and we will all raise our glasses and toast the three of them fighting on the Russian front." It was a grand gesture, but doubts existed within everybody.

It was December 1941, and the snows had come to the Black Forest, making the scenery look even more beautiful. The pine trees were topped with snow as far as the eye could see, and there was a muffled silence that seemed to create a calmness throughout the vast estate. Squirrels could be seen scratching under the surface of the snow, looking for their food buried in the summer, and birds leaving their footprints in the virgin snow somehow enhanced the winter scene even more. The wild deer, more invisible in the summer months, were nervously and carefully walking around the castle grounds, seemingly enjoying the change of environment.

John decided that he and the twins should do some cross-country skiing around the estate as this was the best mode of transport at this time of year, leaving Mary and Angel at the castle to chat.

"Angel, when did you marry and how did you meet Ludwig?" asked Mary.

"I met him in Switzerland while I was on a skiing holiday with my parents. I first noticed this tall man skiing with great skill on the high slopes, and I was impressed. He looked very elegant—the way he moved on the snow. I was an accomplished skier, and he noticed me. When we spoke, he asked if he could buy me a drink, and I accepted the invitation. He was very charming, and we talked for hours. Soon we were spending most of the holiday together.

"Ludwig did not tell me he was the son of a count until we became engaged, so it came as a complete surprise when he casually mentioned that I would become a countess one day. I asked him why he did not mention this to me earlier, and he said that he wanted to make sure that I was not marrying him for the title. How ridiculous is that? I think I knew he was the one for me from the first moment I saw him. We married in Baden—you may have seen the church on your way here from the airport—on 5th September 1911. I remember there were so many guests that many stood outside the church. It was as though the whole town came to celebrate with us. He looked very handsome dressed in his uniform of a young officer.

"I remember my first visit to this castle and how overwhelmed I was by its beauty. Naturally, my parents—now, both deceased—were delighted and saw Ludwig as a perfect marriage partner. After the wedding service, all the guests came back to the castle. We lived in the west wing here until his parents passed away and he inherited his title and the estate.

"Our first child, Dieter, was born one year later, then Heidi, followed by Hans four years after Dieter. Ludwig's father and mother were very happy for us, but his brothers never quite accepted me because I was not nobility and saw me as some kind of gold digger, so we do not see them any more as Ludwig is furious with them.

"They all carry the title of count, but Luds inherited the estate, and that is the real reason for the rift between him and his brothers. Prussian law at that time permitted all sons to keep the title, but only the eldest would inherit the estate. I have no regrets, except that I married a soldier as he is always away from home," she joked.

"That's such a wonderful story, Angel. I met John in 1918 at the hospital where I was working. Poor thing, he looked so sad sitting on the bed in my ward. He had undergone so many operations following his injuries suffered during the war. He did not wear the eye patch then until after he was discharged from the hospital. It was when we got married that he wanted to wear it.

"We were married at Bethnal Green registry office on 26th December 1918, and we lived with John's parents in their house for four years. It was very cramped, but we were happy together, just a few doors from my mum and dad. We started our family in 1922. Unfortunately, there were complications with me having the twins, and we were unable to have any more children. Ludwig has been to our home for the making of the film," Mary said rather nostalgically.

"Mary, you have a wonderful family, and we love you very much." Then Angel rang a servant for some tea. "Did you have a honeymoon?" asked Angel.

"No, money was tight, and John needed money for the business he inherited, but we were happy working hard and raising the family."

Xmas and the New Year of 1942 were celebrated by the two families at the castle; however, the absence of Ludwig was deeply felt, and Angel was having some concerns about his and her sons' safety. She had not received any letters or messages from him for a while. In spite of the propaganda films and newsreels stating that all was well on the Eastern Front, she knew otherwise and was worried.

On 2nd February 1943, twenty-two divisions of the German Army and its Axis allies became encircled by the Soviet Army at Stalingrad after five months of siege of the city. More than 300,000 German soldiers were forced to surrender, including a field marshal and many generals; it was to be the turning point of the war in the East.

Chapter 17

The year 1943 was bleak for the Wehrmacht on the Eastern Front, with their defeat at Stalingrad and the development of new Russian weapons, particularly tanks, such as the T34, that were proving to be more than a match for any tanks used by the panzer units such as Ludwig's.

Ludwig was ordered by Hitler in a desperate attempt to regain the initiative to launch a major offensive against the Bolsheviks and then a final push to take Moscow before the end of the summer; the task faced by Ludwig was formidable. The defeat at Stalingrad had demoralised the entire fighting force of the German Army, and that made Ludwig and his general staff lose confidence that they could win another major battle.

Field Marshall Ludwig Graf Von Klaus had never been on the losing side, but this was different. His men were tired and short of rations and were not the superior force that had overwhelmed Stalin's Red Army at the beginning of the invasion.

What Ludwig did not know was that the Russians were about to launch their own counteroffensive against the German positions, and soon Ludwig's entire army was encircled. Fierce tank battles occurred as the panzer units tried desperately to break-out, but the situation was hopeless as the T34 tanks destroyed one German tank after another.

When Hitler was informed about gravity of the situation, Ludwig was ordered to carry on fighting, as surrender was not to be contemplated. Ludwig, however, had already made the most important decision of his military life—to disobey a direct order—and he surrendered to the Russian forces. He knew what the consequences would be. This way, tens of thousands of German lives would be spared. Yes, they would be prisoners of war, and many would perish, but to sacrifice any of them to save the honour of a maniacal tyrant, such as Hitler, was simply not acceptable to Ludwig.

Ludwig's generals were summoned before the surrender and informed; he wanted a consensus to ensure they were all in agreement. With a heavy heart, the announcement was made. "Gentlemen, our situation is hopeless. The führer has ordered our army group to continue the hostilities against the Russian forces and has forbidden me to, conditionally or unconditionally, surrender. I know you will agree with me when I say we are outnumbered and up against a superior fighting force, and it would be suicidal to continue fighting and sacrifice any more of our brave soldiers of the Wehrmacht who have fought so valiantly. I am, therefore, recommending to each of you that we offer our surrender to the Soviet commander forthwith."

"Ludwig, we have served with you on many successful campaigns, and together we have always shown absolute loyalty to the führer, but now we agree with you, and we must disobey his orders," commented General Ernst Steiner, Ludwig's second-in-command, speaking on behalf of the other generals.

"Thank you, Ernst, for your support. It is a difficult and dangerous decision to disobey Hitler. However, I wanted to make sure you were all in agreement, and you have now confirmed this to me. Hitler's vengeance will be to order our executions. However, we will be away from his clutches in a Moscow prison, but our families in Germany may be at risk from the Gestapo or the SS, so please get messages to them. We must all learn the lessons of Stalingrad and the fate of the commanders after their surrender. It has been an honour to serve with each and every one of you, and I wish you good luck, gentlemen." Ludwig then dismissed his men for the last time.

Now was not the time or place to make inspired speeches. A humiliating surrender for any high-ranking officer of the Wehrmacht was both devastating and dangerous with an uncertain future. Most of the officers who stood before him were friends and had served together since they were young men during the First World War. He knew them well, and some would make the ultimate sacrifice by committing suicide rather than face the shame and humiliation of surrender and captivity.

Chapter 18

Field Marshal Ludwig Von Klaus officially surrendered his army unit of 276,000 men to the Russian commanders on 27th August 1943. A high-ranking officer such as Ludwig was a prize to the Russian hierarchy, and they were quick to make terms with him. Interrogated and imprisoned in Moscow, he awaited his fate but was told that if he cooperated and worked with the Russians, he would eventually be sent home after the war.

Ludwig had no choice if he wanted to see his family again, so he agreed, and to rid Germany of Hitler and the Nazis must be to the good of his country. He asked for three conditions—that he could get a message to his family to inform them that he and his sons were safe, that his two sons and Heinz could re-join him, and lastly, that his men would be treated as humanely as possible as prisoners of war under the Geneva Convention. The Russians agreed. The Soviets were quick to recognise the importance of a field marshal willing to turn against the Nazis in this way, and they responded quickly.

After seeing the Russian propaganda material of Ludwig, Hitler immediately threw into a rage and proclaimed that a death sentence be passed to his former field marshal, but it was all too late, and Hitler could only bluster and was powerless to do anything; Ludwig's family, though, was at risk, and he hoped that John would react as they had discussed.

Ludwig hoped that one day Hitler would be assassinated to shorten the war. Ludwig knew Hitler only too well and was certain that surrender would never be an option for him. He knew that one day if Hitler wasn't assassinated, he would commit suicide, but now, in captivity, Ludwig was powerless to have any direct involvement in the demise of the dictator.

Hitler was still very much in control in Europe, even though the tide was beginning to turn in favour of the Russian Army. By late summer of 1943, his future adversaries—as he saw them—

were only America and the Soviet Union. He had underestimated the Russians and the British. Would he now do the same with the American forces fighting at the moment for the Pacific islands against the Japanese?

When the news of Ludwig and her sons' capture was received by Angel, she was remarkably calm and, in some ways, relieved that her husband and sons were safe. He was a valuable asset because of his status, and she knew the Russian secret service would need to protect him.

She asked the driver to collect Heidi and bring her back to the castle so she could explain the situation personally before telling the others, and after explaining to a very tearful Heidi about her father, they all gathered to hear the news.

For a few moments, everybody was speechless but soon rallied round to console one another. The lady servants all cried for their master, and Angel and Heidi were deeply touched by their outward expression of emotion. Some of the older ones had known the count since he was a baby and had always loved him. The older servants had watched as Dieter and Hans grew into men.

The Groves family was upset too, for Ludwig had saved their lives before, or possibly after the film had been made, and they were extremely fond of him. Mary then said, "I am going to make you all a nice cup of tea." That amused Angel as she knew it was the answer to most problems for the English people. Anyway, it did help to relieve some tension for everybody.

In the Russian detention camp, Ludwig and the others were reasonably well-treated and allowed to write letters. Ludwig was finally allowed to make a vital telephone call to his wife, telling her that they must leave the castle immediately as he had arranged with John. There was no time to lose, and they were prepared and ready to go to the chateau in Switzerland, where they would be safe.

Each visit by the Russian secret service was followed by some verbal pressure for the four prisoners to become communists, and this was skilfully postponed by Ludwig for the others; however, the authorities kept Ludwig informed about events as far as Hitler was concerned, and on one occasion, they told him that his own generals had made a failed attempt on

Hitler's life. This news pleased everybody, including Ludwig's 'guards'.

The guards just happened to be three masculine-looking ladies and had obviously succumbed to Ludwig's charms over the months by giving him extra food, and even wine. This he shared with Dieter, Hans and Heinz. All in all, they were comfortable and well fed in their captivity.

Ludwig had been told a while ago that there were groups of anti-Nazi German prisoners dedicated to expelling the Nazis from Germany. Two committees had been formed; one was called the National Committee, and the other was a Bund Deutscher Offizcere (BDO). This one was for senior officers, and the former was established for the lower ranks.

They were encouraged by the Soviets and given every opportunity to expand the objectives. When Ludwig was approached to join them, he eagerly embraced the idea of the movement and its objectives. He was keen to do everything he could to help; Dieter, Hans and Heinz were just as enthusiastic and wanted to be involved as soon as possible.

The Nazi propaganda machine was swift to denounce Ludwig on the newsreels, accusing him of cowardice and treachery in the face of the enemy. The Gestapo and the SS were ordered by Hitler to arrest his family in a cynical and callous act of vengeance.

Ludwig was one step ahead and had warned his wife well in advance, having secured this condition with the Russians in exchange of cooperating with them. John knew exactly what had to be done, and the two families left the castle several days earlier with Heidi in two cars en route to Switzerland to escape, leaving the servants to stay in Baden Town, where they would be safe.

The journey took about three and a half hours to Zurich and one hour to the family chateau. Poor Angel, throughout the journey she worried if everything had been done. The servants were paid for six months in advance, and Ludwig's two German shepherds were to be looked after along with her four horses by the groom. Angel really wanted to take her dog, Syd, but John advised her against this since the Swiss border guards might enforce the quarantine requirements.

The servants were to return to the castle soon after the Gestapo had left and carry on as normal. One of the two vehicles would return to Baden and come back in six months to collect the servants' wages. The journey from Baden to Switzerland took longer than anticipated. Slowly they were driven over mountainous roads, trying to keep away from main routes to avoid any roadblocks set up by the Gestapo; it was a precaution.

The two cars were heavily laden and had to be carefully driven by the chauffeur and their butler along perilous roads; however, the chauffeur knew their route well, having driven the Von Klaus family to the chateau regularly. When the party finally reached the Swiss border and was allowed to pass through, everyone cheered in both cars, relieved to be safe.

Chapter 19

The chateau was much smaller than the castle but still had sufficient bedrooms for the two families. They had money in several currencies, thanks to Ludwig planning in advance, but Angel's main concern was for the servants' safety and how they would be treated by the Gestapo.

Unbeknown to Angel, Hitler had given orders to the Gestapo and the SS chiefs to be careful not to alienate the people in the Black Forest as he knew the count and countess were highly regarded in the region, but this confusing order cost them time and delay, giving the two families more time to escape.

When the two families had settled at the chateau, John and Mary and the twins were relieved that they did not encounter any German roadblocks and thought how picturesque it all was being located near the mountains. The family used it mainly for skiing when Ludwig was not away. He kept it a secret from everybody outside of the family. He knew that one day it could be useful.

Angel wanted to get a message to Ludwig as soon as possible to stop him worrying about their safety.

"Don't worry, Angel. Ludwig and your boys will be informed that you and Heidi are now safe and well," said John.

"How must Hitler be dealing with all this—from favourite to public enemy within months. However, my Luds will have the last laugh," she replied.

Heidi then asked, "Does this mean that we can never go back to Germany, Mama?"

"No, one day we will return when your father is released, and John and Mary hopefully will be able to safely return to England," Angel replied. "Soon the Americans will liberate both our countries from Nazi tyranny in the West, and the Russians will beat them in the East. It might take some time, but it will happen, Heidi."

John agreed and said, "For now, we must keep a low profile so that few will know we are here."

The Gestapo, with Himmler's SS units, converged on the town of Baden just two days after both families had left for Switzerland. Finding the castle empty after a forced entry, they descended on the town, knocking on every door, seeking information regarding the whereabouts of the Klaus family. Every person they interrogated denied having any knowledge of where they might be, and if they had known, would certainly not divulge anything to the Nazis.

The count and countess were extremely revered in the area, and many of the townsfolk were able to remember Ludwig's father and mother. One very elderly man, as a small child, even had knowledge of Ludwig's illustrious grandparents.

The Schloss (castle) had always played an important role in the town's history. During the last war, the Klaus's allowed it to be used as a convalescent home for injured soldiers of the German Army when the small town hospital became full, and they provided extra money and staff for their families. Ludwig's mother even helped with the nursing.

They had also—going back generations—proved to be a pivot to the well-being of the town and were remembered fondly for their generosity and the support they gave after the Great War when the whole country was impoverished.

Even though their own family fortunes had diminished dramatically, the Klaus's were anxious to provide food—much of it coming from their own estate—to the hard-pressed and starving people of the Black Forest district, even allowing vast plots of land to be used by Baden townsfolk to grow their own vegetables. This was a lifeline to every family in Baden. They knew that the count and his sons were not cowards or traitors, and that he would only surrender unselfishly to save the lives of his men.

Ludwig was still fervently doing whatever he could to denounce Hitler and his Nazi regime, and now the Soviets were almost completely on the offensive. Vast numbers of the Wehrmacht were being taken prisoner, and many had perished or just disappeared. Ludwig always had misgivings about a once-proud army being decimated in this way, and he held Hitler and his henchmen directly responsible for all the war crimes being committed.

The Soviet guards had told him of the massacres of the Russian Jews and ordinary Soviet civilians. "It was a holocaust, and someday the Nazis will be punished for these vile crimes against your people, this I promise you," Ludwig told them, trying his best to hold back his anger and frustration.

Ludwig thought constantly about his wife and daughter and knew they were safely at the chateau in Switzerland. He was so pleased that his friends were also safe and well, and missed everybody so much, but the thought of the war ending and being released from the detention centre and returning to his family in Switzerland and then Germany, kept him going. Instinctively, he was able to assess the situation on the Russian front and was confident that the German Army would be repulsed soon, but much of Europe was still occupied and would take much longer to liberate.

Angel had her moments of melancholy from time to time, and at very bad periods, she would read a letter Ludwig sent to her before going to the Eastern Front.

My dearest Angel,
I am writing this letter from my quarters in Berlin to tell you how much I love you. I may be away from you for a long time and will miss you every day, but my heart will be with you every moment as always.

Someday we will be together again and back to our normal wonderful life that is such a joy for me, and knowing you, Heidi and our sons are safe is the most important thing in my life.
Your devoted husband,
Luds.

Reading the letter always gave her hope for the future and would raise her spirits.

When John, Mary and the twins had settled into their new environment, they began to relax more. Mary's family were by now very homesick and longed to return to England; however, Mary reassured them that one day they would return. Her mother

87

and father both expressed the view they wanted to be buried in England and nowhere else, a sentiment shared by the family.

The twins began further skiing lessons given by Angel, who was still very accomplished, having skied regularly in the wintertime in the Black Forest and on the slopes in Switzerland, but John and Mary preferred much safer pursuits, such as walking and enjoying the wonderful scenery.

Mary's parents would join them, but she always worried because they were in their late seventies and a fall on the ice could be serious; however, Elizabeth also walked with her parents, and she would be an aide for them.

John, however, was harbouring thoughts of returning to England so that he could assist in any Allied landings that might take place, sabotaging key defences originally built to keep the Germans out of England, which now needed to be destroyed.

John thought, *If only I could get to England and join up with one of the resistance movements there.* John was careful not to allow Mary to know his thoughts as, undoubtedly, it would upset her and the twins. Languishing in the safety of a Swiss chateau for years was not what he wanted.

Angel and Heidi worried and missed Ludwig every single day, but there was a glimmer of hope coming out of Russia with news that the Soviet Army was launching more and more counterattacks on the Germans and had great success in repulsing them from their land. Angel was not an admirer of Bolshevism, and in some respects, she was nervous about any invasion of her fatherland. But there seemed no other alternative to rid Germany of the Nazis, and she utterly detested their treatment of the Jews as much as Ludwig did.

Chapter 20

Ludwig and Heinz had now become prominent members of the Free Germany Movement, along with his sons, and all four had been working with the Russian secret service (KGB) to promote subversive activity in Germany.

New plans to assassinate Hitler were now in place, and after each failed attempt, it became harder to succeed because of extra security surrounding the dictator; however, with more and more of the high command desirous of a coup d'état, the task was safer and infinitely more likely.

It had been a year since the attack on Pearl Harbour by the Japanese, and the Americans were now in a position to carry out landings on the British Isles. To liberate its allies from the yoke of Nazism and then to free France would be a massive task involving air, army and naval forces with immense manpower and equipment. Although they were still fighting against the Japanese, the time was right for such an invasion.

The Germans' campaign against the Soviet Union was faltering, and to keep their territorial gains, such as the Ukraine and central parts of Russia, they needed to reinforce their army units by withdrawing large number of soldiers from occupied countries. The Americans, with the British government actively operating from Washington, were fully aware that Germany had started to transfer large contingents of troops from the Wehrmacht and the SS Units in France and England, making it harder to defend their annexed countries.

To guarantee the success of such an invasion would depend on sufficient aircraft carriers and aircraft so that the coastal defences would be destroyed, enabling landings to go ahead with the minimal number of casualties for both the Americans and its allies.

The scourge of the German U-boats had been virtually eliminated, making the Atlantic safe, so dates 4th and 5th August

1943 were decided on. The invasion would include the countries of the British Empire that had not been annexed by the Germans, and their forces would take on a supporting role alongside the Americans.

Subjected to the vagaries of the weather, the landing force was ready. It had crossed the Atlantic with six aircraft carriers and battleships unseen by the enemy, and the British intelligence operating in the USA had confirmed the most suitable and safest places to secure a beachhead. Thankfully, the Luftwaffe was completely and fully occupied on the Eastern Front so that the Allies had superiority of the skies across Western Europe.

Operation Black Swan—as it was so called—started as scheduled with hundreds of the United States Army Special Forces (Green Berets) and airborne division commandos together with Canadian forces being dropped by parachute at the Kent Downs and Sussex Downs and also at Lyme Regis in Dorset, preparing and weakening the German defences along the coast from Lyme to Ramsgate.

Then the landing craft with thousands of marines started their assault on the defending Germans after aircraft from the carriers gave air cover.

It was an unexpectedly easy invasion as the Germans were taken completely by surprise. The Allies sustained few casualties. The American chief of staff and the exiled British government had estimated losses of 5 per cent; however, not even 1 per cent of the Allies had perished, while tens of thousands of Germans were killed or taken prisoner.

It was midday, and the sea was calm, so most of the equipment was landed safely. Some tanks were lost when a few landing craft capsized, but overall, it was a highly successful operation. The Germans had transferred more men from their occupying force, than was anticipated, to the Eastern Front, and now the push towards London would indicate how much and to what extent.

Arriving at the perimeter of London, the Allied force encountered little resistance, with most of the defending Germans surrendering voluntarily. These were not the crack troops that were expected, and it was apparent that the best men had been sent to the Eastern Front, leaving the whole of England weakly defended by young, newly trained Wehrmacht soldiers.

The only real resistance the Allies faced was from the SS units fanatically loyal to Hitler and Himmler, prepared to die for the Reich.

London and parts of England were finally and completely liberated, and the British people celebrated. The hardships and degradation they had suffered were forgotten for a brief moment in time. The Nazis had stretched their forces to the limit, and Hitler would now be regretful that he had taken on such a colossal task of invading the East and the West on two fronts.

The war was not over yet, and plans by the prime minister and his cabinet with its allies were being made for the liberation of France and the rest of Europe. This would become known as the D-Day landings, the largest landing force in the history of warfare.

On 4 June 1944, the Western Allies did indeed successfully land in Normandy, and five beachheads were established, but there were heavy losses. The net was closing in on Hitler; however, there was still much to do to fight against stiff resistance by crack German troops fiercely defending the territory they had initially gained in northern France. The landing crafts were launched from the Dorset coast, as a subterfuge to the Germans who were expecting that the invasion would come from the east coast of England.

When the whole of the British Isles was liberated, the royal family returned to Buckingham Palace, and the British government returned to power. The prime minister then broadcasted an inspiring speech, thanking the nation:

Britain has emerged triumphant from the darkest period in our history, the Nazi hordes have been eradicated from our land, and the people of the British Isles and their allies can be proud of their victory.

The years of suffering and humiliation caused by the excesses of fascism on our soil have now ended, and our people can be praised that they endured in spite of all odds— with courage and tenacity against the Nazi invaders. Soon the whole of Europe will be freed from the tyranny of Nazism, and Corporal Hitler will be held to account.

On hearing the news, John and Mary were jubilant and waited for the day they would be allowed to return home. Angel was so pleased she called for a celebration and said, "My friends, we will all miss you so much. I understand you do want to return home, but I must insist you stay here until it is absolutely safe to return. We can compose a letter to your government, explaining that you were forced to make the propaganda film, and we can obtain a letter from Luds confirming this if it helps. You have money and our full support if you feel it safer to live in a different district in England."

Mary replied, "Thank you and Ludwig for your friendship and help. We will have to go back soon. Whatever the consequences, they will have to be faced." John agreed wholeheartedly.

Chapter 21

The news of the liberation of the British Isles eventually reached Ludwig and his sons, and it was viewed by the sons with mixed feelings. After all, they were Germans, and some loyalty must be towards their fatherland. Ludwig was pleased, for he knew that it would be the only way that the Nazis could be defeated, and that it was a springboard for an invasion of Europe and eventual capitulation of Hitler and the Third Reich. He also thought of his English friends and hoped they would be able to return to their homeland someday.

The four men had been in captivity for two years, and although treated well by their guards at the detention centre, they were always concerned about their fate should the Russians take full control of the Eastern Front, and if they were of no further use in the war effort. The Soviets had suffered much by the Wehrmacht, particularly the SS units, who had committed unimaginable atrocities. Ludwig and the other three inmates feared reprisals against any German prisoners of war by the KGB; it was always on their minds.

Angelika was increasingly concerned that her friends were becoming impatient about their return to London and asked John and Mary if she could write to the British government on their behalf to try to appeal to them for immunity and safe return to Britain. She said jokingly, "I think I learned much from my father in diplomacy, so I will send a letter to the Foreign Office in London in the hope that they will respond in a positive way. I will also ask if anything can be done for Ludwig as well, and plead with them to help obtain his release from Russia."

The letter was sent after full approval by John and Mary.

The Foreign Office
London

To Whom It May Concern,

My name is Angelika Graffan Von Klaus, and I am the wife of General Ludwig Graf Von Klaus.
I am writing to you to ask your forbearance and consideration to allow immunity to John and Mary Groves so they can return to Britain with their family.

They are innocent victims of this terrible war and need to go back to the country they love so much. As a patriot, John risked his life for his country when he established a resistance movement during the occupation of Great Britain by the Nazis. Together with four other partisans, they disrupted a supply train en route to London by removing the tracks. Unfortunately, soon after, two members of John's group were overheard by the Gestapo when they were trying to recruit more members. Interrogated and tortured, they implicated the other members, including John Groves.

My husband became involved when he was ordered to execute an order given by Hitler himself through Joseph Goebbels to make a propaganda film. The recruitment was left to my husband, a general who, at the time, was becoming very disenchanted with the Nazi regime. John's file was shown to him by the Gestapo, and he decided to use John and his family to be featured as the main cast in the film directed by Leni Ribbentrop.

My husband soon realised that while saving John and his family from the Gestapo, he had also endangered their lives by coercing them to make this film. They would be falsely considered as traitors and collaborators by their own countrymen. The general made the decision to harbour the family at our home for their safety as he felt responsible for their dire situation, and they have been with us ever since.

John, for the record, is also a First World War veteran, sustaining serious injuries at the Somme.

After discovering about the Jews being persecuted, Ludwig was even more angry and frustrated with the Nazis but was still loyal to the Wehrmacht, and his last act as a general and, finally, as a field marshal was to command several panzer divisions on the Eastern Front.

He disobeyed a direct order from Hitler himself by refusing to attack superior Russian forces, and surrendered to save the lives of tens of thousands of his own men under his command.

He knew Hitler's vengeance would be swift. He was immediately stripped of all his honours and rank with a sentence of death or ordered to commit suicide.

Ludwig is now a prisoner in a Moscow detention centre and has been cooperating with the Russians to end the tyranny of Hitler and the so-called Third Reich.

I earnestly await your reply and hope you are able to help John, his family and my husband.

Your obedient servant,
Angelika Graffan Von Klaus.

John and Mary both approved the letter. Mary, showing full gratitude, said, "Angel, if that letter does not do the trick, I will be amazed. Thank you so much."

It was several weeks before a reply came back through special diplomatic mail, and it read:

My Dear Countess,

I apologise for the delay in our reply. His Majesty's government is still in the process of organisation after its return from the USA.
Thank you for your letter. The Foreign Office and the War Department have looked at the Groves family's case sympathetically and fully appreciate their situation. John has indeed shown courage and fortitude during a dangerous period and deserves to be repatriated to his own country. His record is exemplary.

Also, we have looked at the possibility that John may be able to assist the war effort by giving us vital information about the Nazi hierarchy.
The RAF will be sending an aircraft to Zürich to arrange for his whole family to come back to London. The flight will arrive the day after tomorrow at noon.

With regards to your husband's plight, this will prove to be difficult since he is in the hands of the Soviets. We can only request for his release, and this could take a long time. But it's not impossible, so please, Countess, do not lose hope.

Please arrange for the Groves family to be at Zürich Airport on time.

Your obedient servant,
Gerald Clifton-Jones.
Assistant to the foreign secretary.

The letter was greeted by the family with great joy at first, but Mary said to Angel a little later that she would miss her deeply and was sorry to leave Angel and her home.

"Thanks all round to Angel for writing such a persuasive and skilful letter," said John. Secretly, though, he was anxious to return home and keen to help further in the war effort.

He had languished in the luxury of the Black Forest and Switzerland too long, while his countrymen had suffered. He had severe feelings of guilt and badly needed to get back to London for his self-esteem.

Angel was delighted for the family, particularly Mary, with whom she had developed a special and enduring friendship. Angel would miss her terribly, but her concerns were for the happiness of the family, and she wished them all well, saying, "I will ring for some champagne to celebrate your good news. We may be short of many things, but our wine cellar is well stocked thanks to Ludwig. You may know he is a collector of rare wines."

Poor Angel, she was trying her best to be happy, but inwardly, she was depressed; she missed her husband desperately, and now her best friends were leaving her. She had feelings and emotions she had never felt before; she would, however, never stand in their way and knew that they would be together again one day.

John then said how sorry they were about Ludwig and said they would do everything they could to help. John was sincere about this statement as he too had forged a special friendship with Ludwig.

Angel replied, nearly in tears, "Now that you have a date to return to London, I have to tell you that following the liberation of Great Britain and then the successful landings by the Allies in France, Hitler ordered the bombing of London in retaliation and vengeance. For several months, unmanned jet-propelled rockets were launched from France, causing devastation to London, particularly the East End, so I hope and pray that your two homes were unaffected. It was broadcast on the wireless in French, but I did not tell you because I knew you would be worried. Now you will soon find out if your homes are okay and not have months or even years of wondering. I am so sorry and hope I did the right thing by not saying anything to you."

Mary replied, "You did, Angel. We would have been worried sick if we had known months ago."

John agreed. "Are they still bombing London?" he asked.

"No, hardly any V2 rockets, as they are called, are getting through. Your brave RAF pilots found a way of tipping the wing tips of the bombs to knock them off course, using their fighter aircraft. Most finished up in the English Channel. The ingenuity of the British never fails to amaze me." Angel was pleased to tell that to them and get it off her chest.

"So these were Hitler's secret weapons and a last-ditch effort. It would take more than that to demoralise Londoners," said John.

A few days later, Angel and Heidi were saying their goodbyes to the family in what was a very moving and emotional farewell. Two cars now awaited to take the family to Zürich for their flight back to Northolt RAF base. Mary had said that she would prefer to say their farewells at the chateau rather than the airport, and Angel agreed.

"It is heartbreaking to leave this wonderful lady and my dearest friend," Mary remarked to John as they walked across the tarmac to board the RAF plane.

Chapter 22

When the family arrived back at Northolt after a few hours' flight, they were warmly greeted by Gerald Clifton-Jones.

"Welcome back to England, my friends. I am Gerald Clifton-Jones, assistant to the foreign secretary. I am delighted to meet you all and have you back safely. You must be tired after your journey. We have two cars to take you back to your homes, so just relax for now. Oh, and please call me Gerald, and I would like to call you John and Mary, if that's okay."

"Yes, that's fine, Gerald," replied John.

When John and Mary were in one of the cars, Clifton-Jones was quick to tell them about the Blitz that had occurred as they drove to Bethnal Green. "My friends, we wanted take you home first so that you can settle in for the night. We have checked beforehand, and it would appear that your street is not damaged by the bombing, I am very pleased to tell you."

"Thank God," Mary uttered.

"I will arrange for a car to collect you both for a debriefing at my office if that's okay, John."

"Yeah, it's fine. Mary and I want to get it over with as soon as possible so we can get back to normal."

"John, there are two gentlemen I would like you to meet tomorrow. They have a proposition for you, but anyway, it can all wait till tomorrow."

John and Mary were thinking of only one thing at this time, and that was their houses. They were both still very apprehensive about what they might find in spite of reassurances by Clifton-Jones.

As they came closer to the East End, they could see the devastation that the rockets had caused. Whole streets were destroyed, and houses were just rubble. There were massive craters where houses once stood. Thankfully, this was something they had avoided courtesy the Von Klaus family.

Mary became very upset as they approached their street. But it was a miracle that it was still intact. The two houses were undamaged; it was such a relief for them.

Clifton-Jones was pleased for them. "I'm very happy for you all. Occasionally, a rocket slips through the net, but soon it will stop completely as the Allies reach the launch places and destroy them. We have to thank a squadron of RAF Spitfire pilots. They actually found a way of tipping the missiles in the air and offsetting their course so they would not land in London. Before that, the wretched V2, as they were known, caused havoc. I will leave you now and see you tomorrow at 10 a.m.," said Clifton-Jones. "Goodbye."

Mary joked and said, "I have three years of housework to do!" And she said goodbye.

John was thinking about the two gentlemen that had a proposal for him and was getting rather excited about it. "It is good to be home, though, without the Nazi presence, Mary."

When John and Mary arrived at Clifton-Jones's office in Whitehall the next morning, they were introduced to the two gentlemen who had been sitting at the end of a large solid oak table. Both were immaculately dressed in smart pinstriped suits, and immediately rose to their feet to shake John's and Mary's hands.

"These gentleman are Anthony and Richard. They only use first names as they are members of a secret organisation set up by the prime minister in 1939 called the Special Operations Executive, or SOE," Clifton-Jones announced.

Anthony, interrupting, then said, "The less we know about one another, the safer it is."

Clifton-Jones then referred to the men as being in charge of all covert operations. "So I will let them explain to you why they have requested to have this meeting, which incidentally has been approved and ratified by us, the Foreign Office, and the War Department."

"Thank you, Gerald." Then Anthony began to address the two who were anxious to know why they were there. "John and Mary, you have had a remarkable three years, and your file is the most bizarre I have ever read. You have met almost everybody in the 'rogues' gallery' of Adolf Hitler, and this makes you a very important asset to our country during this war." He continued,

"Richard and I—with Gerald's help—have been working on a plan to rescue and bring back to Britain, General Ludwig Von Klaus, and with your help, John, we can achieve this. We know you have a unique friendship with him, and we know we must treat the matter with great sensitivity."

John was anxious to interrupt, but thought it more prudent to let Anthony finish.

"John, in short, we would like you to work with us on a special mission to carry out a dangerous operation to bring him to London. Richard and I categorise our missions by colour code: green for 'no danger', amber for 'some risk', red for 'dangerous'. This mission is red, my friend, so we wanted you and Mary to know this. If you agree, you will not be alone as we have two operatives that had been studying the situation there and have reported back favourably."

John answered quickly and said, "Why do you need me if you have others?"

"We will need the general's cooperation in this, but in all probability, we suspect that he will assume it's a German undercover operation by the SS to get him back to Germany for execution and he may not leave. We cannot afford to take that risk as we only have fifteen minutes to carry the rescue out. The general will trust you and go with you straight away without hesitation, so if you do not accept, we will have to cancel our plan. You are our only hope."

Mary was angry. "How can you ask my husband to risk his life again?"

"Mary, we have no other options. The general is such an important figure and the most decorated and highest-ranking officer in the Wehrmacht—or was—so it would be a coup for Britain if we had him here, working with us to shorten the war and save countless lives. He was Hitler's favourite for many years and few know Hitler as well as he does," replied Anthony. Mary was not impressed by Anthony's emotional blackmail but remained silent.

John had listened patiently to Anthony, but asked about his two sons and aide. "Ludwig will not leave the prison unless they go with him. Even I cannot persuade him to do so."

"Yes, John, we have thought about this very seriously and agree with you. It will, however, make the task harder for you and the others so we will leave that to you."

Clifton-Jones then interceded. "We do, though, have another issue that may make the mission harder and more dangerous." He winced and explained, "We cannot have the British government directly involved in this operation since the Soviets would consider it a breach of the terms of alliance with them and endanger relations that are already very tenuous, so I am afraid you and the other partisans will be on your own. Sorry, John."

Clifton-Jones then said that he wanted John and Mary to sign the Official Secrets Act of 1939 before they left the building. "It's just protocol, and now we should stop for some lunch in our canteen—not the best of food. However, there is a war going on, and we should all make sacrifices, don't you think?"

Very pompous, John thought.

Anthony and Richard were anxious to have John's reply but said, "We know it is a very hard decision, and you and Mary will need to discuss through it together, so take your time and get back to us through Gerald if you decide to join us. You have already proved that you are a brave and courageous man, John, so whatever you decide, it will be for the right reasons, and we will respect your decision."

The two gentlemen left the meeting, and after lunch, Clifton-Jones recommenced the meeting by giving John and Mary some good news about the film. "It was never shown in Britain. The Nazis decided at the last minute to cancel it. We are not sure why, but we suspect they were worried about inflaming the British public into more 'subversive' activity. So your family is still anonymous in Britain at least. We know that it was shown to the German public as confirmed by the SOE operatives there, so if you do decide to go on the mission, then you may need to disguise yourself."

John and Mary were relieved to learn the news, of course, and at least they would still be respected in their own country.

"Anyway, how do you feel about the mission?"

John replied instantly, "We both want to help Angelika and Ludwig to be together again with their sons as a family in Switzerland, and to help shorten the war and save lives would make me a happy man. But I also have to think of my own family too, so the decision to go will have to be with the consent of Mary and my twins," said John, quite composed. Secretly, he was excited about the prospect.

Clifton-Jones replied, saying, "I know the general has never been a Nazi and is a good and honourable man. However, he will, inevitably, have to face the International Court of Justice after the war and will be tried as a war criminal because of his rank and earlier relationship with Hitler, but if we have him in Britain, working with us, then there will be leniency if he is found guilty. I am not sure if the countess is aware of this, and I must ask you not to speak or communicate with her until the matter is resolved. You will have to be careful after signing the Official Secrets Act."

These bloody civil servants, John thought to himself.

Chapter 23

Clifton-Jones was anxious to further explain, to John how important it was for the war effort that the general is interrogated by British intelligence, and he continued, "John, for some years now, we have been pursuing and bombing targets in an effort to locate and destroy the sites and factories where the rocket-propelled missiles are being produced. It's code-*named Operation Crossbow*. You have already seen the devastation they can cause. We must stop the production of any jet propulsion by the Nazis as there may be more weapons of destruction in the pipeline.

"The general may be able to help us significantly on this by passing on information about where the rockets are produced and stored. We know originally they were developed in an area in northern Germany called Peenemunde at a scientific development centre on the Baltic coast. We bombed this site in August 1943, but regretfully, the raid was ineffective, and since then the Americans have tried three times unsuccessfully.

"British intelligence has revealed that the Nazis have moved to another site known as Nordhausen, also in the north. We are hoping that the general can give us detailed information on the whereabouts and the type of construction of the factories. We fear though, and suspect that by bombing the overhead targets, we have forced them to tunnel underground, and the consequence of this is that the SS will be using forced labour from a local concentration camp as was the case at Peenemunde. Thousands of lives will be lost in the most dreadful way as they will be working and sleeping underground in the most squalid conditions imaginable, and if we can stop production of the rockets, we can stop the bombing and save the lives of countless number of Londoners."

For the first time, John heard real passion in Clifton-Jones's voice, and he replied, "If I do go on this mission, I will do

104

whatever I can to get the general back here in this very office, I promise you that."

"John, the prime minister has expressed how important it is to have the general here in London. The German scientists that have been working on these projects are vital for the future development and safety of the empire against those who would seek to wage war against us in the future. After the Nazis have been defeated, it will be vital that the scientists do not fall into the hands of the Soviets. We must have them working for the West at any cost. Many are Nazis but will be given immunity against any indictments they would face if we have them either here or in America. British and American intelligence have discovered that the general knows personally many of the leading scientists and can name them and persuade many to come to the West and continue their work, so more pressure on you, I'm afraid," concluded Clifton-Jones.

He then brought the meeting to a close and stated he looked forward to seeing them again soon. "Another meeting will be held if you decide to join the SOE."

When the couple were alone and back at their house, John pleaded with Mary to have her approval. He wanted her to say something to encourage him by giving her blessing for him to go, and he was very persuasive by saying, "Mary, you have been very quiet. I need to know how you feel about this if I decide to go."

"I think you have already made up your mind, John, so it doesn't really matter what I say. I do want the Von Klaus family to be together again, but what of my family if you fail to come back to us? I'm petrified, John, at the thought of losing you."

"Mary, thank you. You know I must do this for my own self-respect. I have hated myself ever since we made that awful film. Living in luxury, while our friends and neighbours were desperately short of everything and having to suffer while the Nazi scum invaded their homes, has made me ashamed. I will never forgive myself for accepting that blood money from Hitler. I will phone Clifton-Jones tomorrow and arrange a meeting with the SOE. You do know that we cannot say anything to the twins, Mary, or your family?"

"Yes," said Mary very tearfully.

Chapter 24

Everybody at the Foreign Office was pleased at John's acceptance, and the planned mission was revealed by Anthony and Richard in the presence of Clifton-Jones. Mary did not attend the meeting, as requested by the SOE officials since it would be too distressing for her to listen to the details of the mission. She was also informed that any outstanding bills that needed to be paid would be met by the Treasury—and there were many after three years away.

SOE began the meeting by thanking John for his acceptance to join them in this vital mission and the importance of keeping it classified as top secret.

"A Lysander aircraft will take you to Allied-occupied France in two weeks, leaving from Tangmere air base in East Sussex. This will give us time for some training with weapons and parachute drops. Richard will coordinate this into the schedule, and we expect you to stay at our training camp and not go home after tomorrow.

"An RAF aircraft will take you to the drop zone outside the Russian border in Poland, as we cannot take the risk of flying into Russian airspace. Sorry about this, John, but you will be a long way from the prison in Moscow. It's actually more than five hundred miles from the prison. However, your co-operatives have a planned route to get you there. This will be the most dangerous part of the mission as you may encounter German units.

"The general and the others exercise on their own, around the perimeter fence. The guards usually leave them to their own devises, we have noticed, usually at 14.00 hours. There is a wooded area with good cover at the northern end of the fence. You and your team have fifteen minutes to cut the fence and get the general and the others out before they are missed and the guards are alerted.

"I must say that the security for such a high-profile prisoner is fairly relaxed, and I suspect that the guards have become complacent after three years."

"The general is a real charmer and probably had the lady guards eating out of his hand, knowing him as I do," quipped John.

"Well, that's one of the reasons we wanted you for this mission—you know him so well," said Anthony.

Continuing, Anthony explained about the fence. "As far as we know, it is not electrified, so this will not be a problem. Your job is to persuade—as we mentioned before—the general to leave with you and reassure him and the others that it is in their best interest to get to Britain." Anthony continued his briefing with John. "There will be seven of you to make your escape, and the two partisans with you have studied the route back in great detail. It will be dangerous, though, because—as I said before—when you leave Russian soil and enter Poland, an area occupied by the Germans, the risks are high and cannot be overstated.

"One of your partisans, called Etienne, has been with the French Resistance since 1939 and has collaborated with the SOE since we were formed. He is the one with the knowledge of the area. Mark, our very own operative, is our weapons-and-explosives expert. And, John, you can trust these men with your life. You could not be working with a better team. They are our best operatives.

"When you have completed your objectives, Etienne will drive his van to take you to northern France—now occupied by the Allies. And from there, another aircraft will fly you back to Tangmere air base, and your mission will be complete. Do you have any questions, John?"

"What happens to Ludwig when you have him in London?"

"He will be debriefed and held in custody until the war is finished, and I promise you personally that he will be treated with the utmost respect that his rank deserves. Here at the Foreign Office, we have special holding cells for special prisoners, so the general will be comfortable along with his sons and aide. You will have access, John, to see him whenever you wish. That will be better for him so that he does not feel alienated."

Anthony then concluded his part of the meeting and passed John over to Richard, who would arrange for his training.

"John, I will collect you from your house at 06.00 hours tomorrow and take you to Tangmere air base for your pre-training programme. We have planned the mission to start on 22nd August, so we have eight days to get you into shape, John," Richard said slightly jovially. "We will have that forty-seven-year-old body looking like a thirty-year-old."

John laughed and said, "Without sounding flippant, I am at this moment more worried about the training than the mission."

Mary Anne, James and Mary's family were told that John was working for the Foreign Office and would be away for a few weeks so as not to worry them, but Mary knew the truth and had to keep a brave face, particularly for the twins. They had all been banned from knowing the truth because of the sensitivity and secrecy of the mission.

That night seemed quite normal, except for Mary and John, who knew that maybe it could be their last evening together. Mary, although still angry, did her best to conceal it for John's sake. The next morning, John was ready to be collected at 06.00. He knew these people were always punctual, and they were, that very morning.

John and Mary had said their goodbyes and expressed their love for each other. They had always been very devoted; however, the circumstances made the couple become even closer, and both were emotional. Before closing the front door, John's last words to Mary were, "Don't worry. I will return to you, darling."

Chapter 25

Very soon after arriving at Tangmere, John started his training course under the direction of Richard and the trainer known as Jock. He was very heavily built and spoke in an unusual Scottish accent. The first few hours was just running with the trainer, and as the day wore on, it became more intense. The equipment over John's shoulders became heavier, and by lunchtime, it felt as though John was carrying bricks.

The afternoon came as a welcome relief when weapons training was given, and John did feel much more comfortable with this; it reminded him of the trenches during the First World War. The next day came the part he was dreading most—the parachute training. But after the initial jump, John was more relaxed and ready to do a drop from an aircraft the following day. These procedures seemed endless; however, on the eighth day, John was told he was now ready for the mission that had been code-named *Black Hole,* and was given his equipment.

On 22nd August, as scheduled, John boarded the Lysander that carried just the pilot and himself, and left for France. There he was to be briefed for the next leg of the journey by another SOE man and flown to Paris, which had just been liberated by the French Resistance.

After being flown to the Polish border by the RAF, he finally reached the drop zone and made his rendezvous to make contact with Mark and Etienne.

John parachuted into the rendezvous area about half a mile away from the actual meeting point, and his two counterparts arrived fifteen minutes later to greet him enthusiastically.

Mark spoke to him first, saying, "Welcome, John. I am Mark—the clever one—and this lunatic is Etienne." He laughed.

Etienne gave both men a big smile and replied, "You have to have a sense of humour on these missions as it helps to combat the fear, but it is good to meet you, Monsieur."

Quickly folding John's parachute, all three men went into Etienne's van to have some food and drink, and discuss the plans. And of course, they were vigilant just in case they had been seen by the Germans.

"How dangerous is this area?" John asked.

Etienne replied, "Not too bad here. This part of Poland strangely is not infested by Nazi scum, but where we are going towards the camp, things could be different. We may encounter German units in that area, so we must be careful not to be seen by any."

They then started to discuss the plan. Mark said, "We should leave early tomorrow as it will take about nine hours, at least, to reach our target."

"That's fine with me, gentlemen. The sooner we get it over with, the better," replied John. Etienne wondered if John needed more rest. John replied, "No, I will not sleep anyway, so we can get a really early start tomorrow morning at first light."

"John, we know our reasons for going on this mission, but how about you? We hear you are friends with the German general," asked Mark.

"Yes, we first met under strange circumstances. However, he is not a Nazi, and he wanted to be involved in Hitler's assassination. He surrendered his panzer units to the Russians on the Eastern Front, and that is why he is in Russia now. But it is a long story, so we will have to leave it there." John was cautious not to say too much about Ludwig.

"We also heard that the Allies are making good progress and Paris has been liberated and soon Holland will follow," stated Mark.

"Etienne, you must be so pleased. Do you have family there?" asked John.

"Yes, I am a Parisian, and it is a real morale booster—as you English say. But I think there is still much to do."

"That's right, and that is why it is so important to safely get the general back to London. He could shorten the war and save so many lives," said John very passionately.

The three men took turns to keep guard during the night, in case German units were about. Tomorrow would be crucial and very long. John thought of his family and prayed silently that he would see them again.

At 04.00 hours, the group was awake and bound onwards for the prison camp. Etienne was driving, John was a passenger and Mark at the rear was fully armed in case they encountered German patrols.

They had a radio receiver, three rifles and pistols, hand grenades and three machine guns—all of which, John hoped, they would not have to use. They had no papers and did not need them in the circumstances they were in since they all knew the risks of being shot on sight should they meet any Germans.

"Etienne, where are the concentration camps in Poland?" asked John.

There was a long pause before Etienne spoke, and it was obviously very sensitive to him. "The nearest from where we are now is one they call Belsen. It is about 300 kilometres from here. My mother was taken to one, that I believe is this. She is Jewish and was taken from us when the Nazis invaded Paris in 1940. My father died from a broken heart soon after, and I do not know if my mother is alive or not. I think of her every day, and it hurts." Etienne struck his chest.

John was annoyed with himself for asking the question and upsetting Etienne, so he offered his apologies.

"No, don't be sorry. It's okay, but now you know why I play such dangerous games, Monsieur," he joked, trying to be more sanguine about it.

John then asked Mark why he joined the SOE.

"My family are Jewish and were all taken by the Nazis after the invasion of Britain. They were sent to detention camps for over a year and were released by the liberating forces. My parents have never been well since and find it hard to talk about their experiences, so I don't ask. But my two brothers and sister are now okay and want vengeance as I do. We can never forgive, and that is why I risked my life for my family. I was lucky to be not in our house in Whitechapel at the time, but that awful day, when I came home from work and saw the word *Juden* painted in red on our front door and discovered my parents had been taken will live with me for the rest of my life."

Mark appeared to be relieved that he had told the two men. John now clearly understood the reasons his two brave colleagues were able to risk their lives day in and day out; his was just a one-off mission and would be over soon, hopefully.

His respect for Etienne and Mark was enormous. *And if my mission fails, my participation with these men will not have been in vain,* he thought.

After three hours of driving, John took over from Etienne. The van was similar to his own back home, and it made a pleasant change, for he had not driven his for some years.

Two hours had passed when, suddenly Etienne spotted a German patrol going in the opposite direction. Would they stop? It was a tense moment for the group as there were about six vehicles carrying soldiers of the Wehrmacht with some motorcyclists. They were outnumbered should there be a confrontation.

"What a relief—it isn't stopping," Mark announced as the patrol passed by. "This means we are getting closer to our destination. I would say about five and a half hours of normal drive time, and we should be there before 13.00 hours. It's better not to be hanging around the camp too long," he continued. "I'll take over the driving now, John. You can be on guard in the back."

As John sat in the back of the van, he noticed how organised these two were—ample food and drink, plenty of spare petrol and blankets. The wire cutters were ready to make an opening to allow the general and his party to escape through the fence. It was indeed well planned, and they both knew it.

"You chaps are so organised," John said.

"We don't leave anything to chance, John. A small mistake or omission could easily cost us our lives," Mark admitted.

"It's good to be working with such professionals," said John.

"Don't forget to tell Anthony and Richard how good we are so that we can be honoured," Mark joked.

"Of course I will, gentlemen," replied John rather sarcastically.

Suddenly, without warning, a German motorbike and sidecar pulled alongside and ordered Mark to stop their vehicle. While one German held a machine gun, the other asked for their identity papers. Mark was pretending to search while the other German went to the back of the van and opened the door, but John was ready and immediately fired a round, killing the inquisitive German immediately. Meanwhile, Mark fired at the other German, killing him as well.

They needed to hide the dead Germans and be on their way, so they quickly dumped the bodies in the undergrowth at the side of the road, covering the motorcycle as well and drove on to their destination.

"Where did they come from!" asked Etienne.

"It was probably from the patrol that went by half an hour ago," Mark replied. "Was that your first kill, John?" asked Mark.

"Yes, and I feel sick. Can we stop for a minute?" John was about to vomit.

"Sorry, John, we can't stop. We have lost nearly an hour. Use this bucket," said Etienne.

After John was sick, he felt better and apologised, "Sorry, gents. I feel okay now."

"That's normal, John, with your first kill. It's a shock, but well done. Your reactions were good and saved our lives," said Mark, continuing to drive.

"I would like to kill a Nazi for every Jew they have murdered in the camps," Etienne remarked. Etienne then urged Mark to drive faster. "There may be more German patrols ahead, so we must be vigilant. The two men will be missed, *mes amis*."

"Thank goodness I had the weapons training. These new machine guns are so different to the old rifles we used during World War I at the Somme," said John, recovering well. The incident had further increased the camaraderie between the men, and trust—so necessary during dangerous missions—was now definitely confirmed.

They had driven for many hours without further incident and were now in Russian territory. The time had arrived after many more hours of driving to fulfil their objectives. The three men were on the other side of the woodland. A short distance from there was the final spot to liberate the four people from the camp. All the planning and discussions had now reached reality, and John just hoped the general would be true to form and leave with him.

As they reached the fence, they were pleased that no patrols were apparent. This would make work safer and easier than anticipated. It was 13.50 hours when they saw the four men approaching the intended escape route through the fence that had been neatly opened with the cutters by Mark.

When they were close enough and within earshot, John called out to Ludwig, "Luds, it's John. We have come to help you, your sons and Heinz to escape from here and take you back to England." John had deliberately used his nickname so that Ludwig would know it was a close friend calling. "You must be quick before your guards notice you are missing."

Ludwig was overwhelmed, but he composed himself rapidly, calling to his sons and Heinz to leave through the fence immediately. He said, "It is my friend John, and you can trust him."

They wasted no time and were soon in the van, driving away from the prison. "We must get out of Russia and cross the border and into Poland quickly. When the guards discover you are missing, Ludwig, this area will be swarming with Russians, but I want to tell you that these men I am with are totally trustworthy and professional, so we have a great chance to escape."

"John, I can't believe you have all risked your lives to liberate us. Thank you."

John thought that Ludwig looked much thinner and asked if he was okay.

"It has been difficult for the last three years, but we are all fine and missing our family. How are Angel and Heidi? Are they well?"

"Yes, Ludwig, we saw them a short while ago just before we left Switzerland for England, but I must tell you that you will not be able to go back to Switzerland yet to see her immediately. The British government wants to debrief you and help them in the war effort. I promise, you will be well looked after, and we can arrange to have Angelika and your daughter flown to London. The Foreign Office will do whatever they can to help if you cooperate with them."

"Of course, I will. I want to see that tyrannical Nazi dictator dead and buried and the war over. I have thought about this continually during my captivity."

Meanwhile, the priority was to make good their escape from Russia and then Poland. It would be another eleven or so hours of driving, and the two men had lots to talk about.

"Heinz, it's good to see you again."

"Yah, you too, John."

Ludwig's sons remained silent and suspicious about their rescuers. After all, they had not met John before and obviously needed time.

Etienne had taken a different route back. It was slower but mostly under the cover of the trees to evade detection from Russian aircrafts, and it seemed to be working since they arrived and crossed over the frontier into Poland.

Etienne had certainly managed to evade the Russians, but could he do the same with the Germans? They had a long way to go; however, John, Mark and Etienne were all confident they would reach the safety of the Allied-occupied territory, and, miraculously, they did.

Ten hours later and several different drivers, the tired and wary men arrived safely in France without incident, for their flight by the RAF back to England. Mark and Etienne were requested to return as well to be debriefed, and the mission was accomplished.

The general expressed his relief at arriving safely back, remarking, "It must have been by divine intervention, gentlemen, and by your courage that we have returned safely."

Chapter 26

John's priority was to let Mary and the children know that he was back safely and would be home that very evening. Mary was so happy, and could not wait to see her husband. She knew that the Foreign Office would need to debrief John about their successful mission. Moreover, she wanted to see Ludwig too, hoping that they would arrange for Angel and Heidi to visit them in London. However, she had to be patient and was anxious to tell the twins and her family that John was back.

Ludwig was technically in custody, along with his sons and Heinz, and waited to be interrogated by Anthony, Richard and Clifton-Jones—but not before the accolades and acknowledgments to the three men that had made *Black Hole* a successful mission.

John then asked Clifton-Jones to arrange for the general's wife and daughter to be collected and flown to London as he had promised Ludwig as part of the conditions to get him to London—a little white lie but so important for Ludwig's trust and cooperation. This was agreed and would be arranged in a couple of days.

The Foreign Office was bending backwards to accommodate their prized capture, and John wanted to take full advantage for Angel and Ludwig's sake as he had promised. It would also help to gain the trust of his sons too and, of course, Heinz.

Clifton-Jones was keen to start debriefing everybody. He knew, though, that tomorrow they would have rested, so he scheduled the following day at 09.00 hours as the meeting time.

Mary's reunion with John was emotional. She thought, at times, she would never see him again.

"Mary, I told you I would return, my darling. And have you noticed how fit I look after the training I did? And the parachute jumps—so exciting!" John said proudly.

"John, you must promise me that it was your last venture. I don't think I could cope with you doing that again," pleaded Mary.

"It was my last, and I feel that I have regained my self-respect. Anthony and Richard will not talk me into another mission. All the ole boys in the world will not persuade me. I will do my very best for Ludwig and Angel though. They will need us, Mary. Clifton-Jones has already told me that Ludwig will have to face the International War Crimes Committee after the war. The British government will do what they can to support him as he has promised his full cooperation."

There were hugs all around when the twins returned home after work. Mary Anne and James were both working at the hospital where their mother was still a nurse. John did not mention the killing of the two Germans, and never would. He felt it prudent not to alarm Mary with the real dangers of the mission, and he wanted to forget that it had occurred.

John had formed a bond with Etienne and Mark as a result of his affiliation with the SOE and wanted them both to join him when he had the opportunity to see his friend Ludwig again to get to know him better, and they agreed. The best time would be after the meeting that was about to start.

Clifton-Jones started by thanking the SOE team for their part in rescuing the general from the Russians and getting him to London. "I think it is appropriate now to ask General Von Klaus to join us."

The general entered the room and immediately thanked everybody for his freedom from Bolshevik captivity. "Gentlemen, I am grateful to you all, particularly to John, Etienne and Mark for risking their lives to give me the opportunity to see my wife and daughter again. I know I will have to face trial for war crimes because of my rank and past, but I was vehemently against the Nazi ideology and the treatment of the Jews and will regret, till the end of my days, that I did not do enough to stop the tyrannical regime from slaughtering millions." Ludwig was contrite and sincere. "For the wicked crimes of my country and my earlier involvement with the Nazis, I wish to atone and will do anything in my power to assist you."

"General, I thank you for coming to London and will help you through the difficult days that lie ahead for you and your family. Your full cooperation to give any information relating to Hitler and the regime will assist us to secure your release completely, but meanwhile, in a couple of days, you will be reunited with your wife and daughter, and arrangements have been made. John has told us how much you have done for his family, and although we are obliged to hold you and your sons in custody, we don't want you to feel like prisoners here. If there is anything you need, please ask," Clifton-Jones answered sincerely.

After a long debriefing, John, Etienne and Mark went to see Ludwig, and John told him how happy he was to see him again. "Ludwig, I thought it would be a good idea for Etienne and Mark to meet you as they have bitter memories of the treatment given to their families in the concentration camps. It may help them if you answer some of the questions that they have. Do you agree?"

"Yes, John. Ask of me what you will, gentlemen."

Mark was first to ask. "When did you find out about the death camps in Poland?"

"Hitler never informed me. It was a conversation with a high-ranking SS officer in 1942, in Berlin, that I found out when he began to boast about the 'Jewish solution' that Himmler had planned. I found it abhorrent and was sickened by it, and I decided at that point to be part of the organisation to assassinate Hitler, known as the Free Germany Movement. Unfortunately, before I could actively get involved, I surrendered to the Red Army. You know the rest of the story."

"Why did you join the Wehrmacht, and did you ever respect Hitler?" asked Etienne.

"My father was a soldier, and it seemed to be a natural thing for me to join the army. There was none of this Nazi nonsense then, and I wanted to do my best to help Germany recover from the First World War. Like all other young men of the German officer corps, I was carried away with the fervour, and Hitler at that time seemed like an inspirational leader to steer Germany back to prosperity. So we followed him and soon the economy of Germany was raised and the people felt good about themselves. He had enormous support from the Wehrmacht and the other institutions as a saviour of Germany. We were all blind to the reality of the murders and killings during the early days of any opposition against Hitler and the Nationalist Party.

"Hitler's obsession with Bolshevism lost the war for Germany way back in 1942 when Barbarossa was launched and the Wehrmacht support drifted away. Yes, Etienne, I did respect him until I found out what the Third Reich really stood for. I should have read *Mein Kampf*. The evils of Hitler's ideology were there, staring all of Germany in the face, but we never took any notice until it was too late."

"Thank you for your frankness, general," said Etienne.

"I am not a general anymore, so please call me Ludwig."

The three men left Ludwig and would meet again soon with Anthony and Richard at another meeting.

Anthony seemed to be in a jubilant mood. "Good morning, gentlemen of the SOE. Yesterday I was called to the War Cabinet Rooms for an update on the current situation on the war by the prime minister. The Allies are making good progress. Over three hundred thousand soldiers of the British Expeditionary Force taken prisoner in 1940 have been freed, and many will be joining combat units if they are fit to do so. Most of France has been liberated, and on the Eastern Front, Jerry has lost control of most of their previously occupied territory in Russia, and are being pushed back into Poland.

"There is still much to do, however, and the War Department are receiving reports that the Germans have launched a major counteroffensive in the Ardennes region of France, Belgium and Luxembourg, a few days ago on 16th December. It would seem that German re-enforcements are being diverted from the Eastern Front to the Western Front, so I am afraid that victory is still many months away and we must soldier on—pardon the pun.

"The prime minister and his war cabinet were delighted to hear our news that General Ludwig Graf Von Klaus will be collaborating with Britain and reaffirms his full support to do whatever needs to be done. He also is grateful to the three of you for risking your lives in bringing the general to London and—wait for it—has recommended you all for honours. He said the importance of having the general in our hands cannot be underestimated, and your achievements must be recognised at the highest level with the George Cross—"

Before Anthony had even finished, a loud cheer came from the three men.

"I can't believe it! All these years, I have been operational, and now this," said Mark in utter disbelief.

Etienne followed. "Messieurs, how can this be? I am French."

And John was humbled that the prime minister of Great Britain should even mention his name. "I am so proud," he uttered, hardly able to speak. "What is the George Cross?" John asked.

Anthony explained, saying, "It is one of the highest awards for a civilian and is equivalent to the Victoria Cross. If you were in the military, you would have been awarded with VCs."

Richard was also very excited and told them that they deserved this award. He quipped, "I am extremely jealous, you know. You will meet the king at Buckingham Palace, and he will present your medals."

Anthony concluded that it was an honour for the SOE. "This will silence our critics, who say we have not been successful. I think this calls for a glass of champagne, don't you, Richard?"

"Yes, ole boy, I'll get the glasses."

"God save the king," Anthony declared.

Chapter 27

The Germans had indeed launched a major offensive in the Ardennes region of France, Belgium and Luxembourg, and it was a temporary setback for the Allies. It became known as the Battle of the Bulge and lasted over six weeks with great loss of life, and the USA bearing the brunt.

The Germans were finally defeated in this battle on 25th January 1945. With such a loss of men and equipment, they would never be able launch another counteroffensive again.

Ludwig was anxious and longed to see his wife again. It had been the longest and saddest time they had been apart. Even as a soldier fighting in campaigns away from home, it had never been so stressful. At times, he was heartbroken and missed her so much.

Angel was the love of his life, and he would do anything to see her again. Mary and John knew this and were determined to make it happen. John had been very firm with his demands to do the mission that the British government would arrange to collect Angel and Heidi from Switzerland.

So on 22nd December 1944, Ludwig would have the best Christmas ever as Angel and Heidi appeared before him in his room in the Foreign Office. The emotional scene that followed was overwhelming. A few minutes later, Dieter and Hans arrived, and the family reunion was complete.

John had asked Clifton-Jones if he would agree to allow the Von Klauses to spend Christmas Day with his family, and he said, "Of course, the general has given us so much useful information over the past month. How can I refuse? I am afraid though they will have to stay in the building in one of our large rooms."

John had told Mary and the twins about the George Cross and that they might need to go to Buckingham Palace, but they had all thought it was just one of his jokes, and it took a while to convince them.

Mary immediately panicked and said, "What will I wear, John, if I am introduced to the royals?"

"I am sure you will find something. If not, we will buy you a new dress. We can afford it now, as Anthony has offered me a job at the SOE. Not sure what I will be doing yet, but they do want me."

"As long as you don't go on any more missions!" she replied.

"No way, Mary. I have told him and Richard that if I do accept their offer, it will be to help in the planning and organisation of London. I think Richard wants me as an assistant, and he knows I will refuse any field missions."

Mary Anne and James expressed their pride and joy that their father was a hero, and Mary's parents and sister were ecstatic upon hearing the news. Meanwhile, they were just pleased to be together, hoping they could spend some time over Christmas with Angel, Ludwig and their family. For the time being at least, the worst was over.

Meeting Angel again was such a joy for Mary; she had missed her terribly, and spending Christmas with her and Ludwig meant so much. She had noticed a physical change in Ludwig; he was slimmer and paler from what she remembered, but this was what one would expect from being incarcerated for three years. However, he was still dashing and handsome and had not lost that charm.

Heidi was as usual effervescent and full of energy, but her two brothers were different and less friendly towards Mary and John.

Ludwig said quietly, "Don't worry, they will come around. They're not so happy as we are to be in London."

"How is Heinz, Ludwig? Is he well?" asked Mary.

"Heinz is always well, thank God. I seem to rely on him more and more these days. While we were in detention, he was an enormous support for me—more so than my sons, I regret to say. What will happen to him after the war, I cannot say, but I really hope he doesn't face a war crimes prosecution. I will try to protect him."

"Is he married?" asked Mary.

"No, he has been a soldier and spent years with me."

"I am certain you will look after him, Ludwig, as though he were one of your family."

They then went to a specially prepared room at the Foreign Office to enjoy the Christmas festivities. The main topic of conversation was John's award, and Ludwig proposed a toast. "To my special friend and saviour, John Groves, a very brave and honourable man to whom I owe so much. Congratulations and thank you for risking your life and bringing my family together. Thanks to you, Mary, for agreeing with John on this. I know if you had said no, he would not have gone to Russia." And they all raised their glasses, wishing one another "Merry Christmas."

After dinner, John asked Ludwig, "Would you have left the camp if I had not been with the others?"

Ludwig answered candidly, "No, I would not have left with them. Etienne is French, and I could not risk being captured by the French Resistance. I recognised that Mark was a Jew, and that would have posed an even bigger risk for myself and my sons and Heinz. There is an active organisation working underground to capture high-ranking Germans for execution, so when I saw you, I had no worries at all and knew you would be working for the British government. Why do you ask?"

"Sometimes I feel like a fraud, Ludwig, and have doubts in my mind if I deserve all these accolades. Now you have said this, I feel a lot better." John had been doubting himself and the answer that Ludwig gave was what he had wanted to hear. "Oh, Ludwig, I have some news. Anthony has offered me a job within the SOE as Richard's assistant, so I will be at the Foreign Office mostly, and will be able to watch over you," he joked.

"That is good news indeed," Ludwig replied, trying to sound very English and getting a little drunk. "Remember, my friend, your work with your own resistance movement before SOE. Nobody can forget that, and your prime minister certainly hasn't."

"Mary, we owe you and John so much for what you have done for my family. You have reunited us, and we are so grateful to you both. I have one more dream—to return to my beloved home in Baden. Luds will not let Heidi and I return until the Nazis are defeated. He insists it is too dangerous and that we must stay in London or Switzerland. Heidi is anxious to get back to work, and I need to see my staff to make sure they are all okay. I miss them terribly, and as you know, they are like an extended family to us," remarked Angel.

"Angel, I agree with Ludwig. It would be risky even to travel there, so please don't go. You must wait until the end of the war, and it is only a matter of months now, according to John. Then we can get back to normal life again," replied Mary.

"Yes, darling, you are right. You always are," answered Angel. "Great news about John's new appointment with the Foreign Office and, of course, his honour. We are all proud of him. And meeting the king—well, that is special, Mary. Luds's honours mean very little to him now as they were awarded to him by an evil man. My husband is very contrite and will never wear them again," said Angel ruefully.

Chapter 28

On 1st January 1945, the George Cross awards to John, Mark and Etienne were officially announced, and a date was set for the medals to be presented by the king at Buckingham Palace. There was great excitement within John's family and some confusion about what to wear for this occasion.

Clifton-Jones gave the best advice and said, "Royal protocol is very subjective on these occasions—for men, morning suits with hat and, for women, long dress with hat. Although we are in 1945, the rules are clear and strict, so I hope this helps you all. I will be at the palace with you, and the prime minister will attend and has indicated he would like to meet you, Mark and Etienne to congratulate you personally."

The presentation followed two weeks later; it was such a grand occasion, and John was nervous throughout. He recalled the last time he was at the palace; it was when the swastika flag was flying, and he had asked Ludwig to remove it.

Mary seemed more relaxed being in the company of the royal family and articulated well, particularly when the queen asked her about her nursing career.

The queen seemed really interested and asked, "How long have you been nursing, Mrs Groves?"

"Nearly thirty years, Your Majesty," she said after she curtsied.

"So you have nursed soldiers during two wars. What an achievement for you."

"Thank you, Your Majesty."

The king asked John if he was a First World War veteran, and he replied, "Yes, Your Majesty. I was injured and was unable to return to the front line."

"So this award is a little overdue, and certainly well earned," said the king.

After the medal ceremony, John was presented to the prime minister, who said. "You and your fellow operatives of the SOE have made an immense contribution to the war effort, and getting the general to London without an international incident was a major achievement. The empire owes you a great debt, and the general has already given us information that will help to shorten this war. So well done and good luck."

John had always admired the prime minister's oratory skills and was not disappointed upon hearing the great man speaking to him personally. It was not hard to realise why the British people stood firm against the Nazis during the dark days of occupation. Even speaking from America, he was able to inspire the country.

Meeting the other recipients of awards after, John was emotional and could not believe he had just met and spoken to the most important people in Britain. They all shook hands and were somewhat relieved it was all over.

Etienne was first to comment. "Mon ami, I spoke to the British king and the prime minister."

Mark said he was proud the way they have been so supportive to the Jewish people around the world, and the prime minister announced to him, "The Soviets have entered the Auschwitz concentration camp, and shortly the British Army will be liberating the Bergen-Belsen camps, so we are close to victory and the destruction of Corporal Hitler's so-called Third Reich."

This was fantastic news for both Mark and Etienne; Mark could now hope that his parents could now find solace, and Etienne wondered if his mother was alive and well too. Both men shook hands, and John was happy for them. But he had doubts; the information coming from British intelligence was that it had been described as a holocaust, with millions of Jews being slaughtered in these camps of death.

Following all the excitement at Buckingham Palace, John reported for duty to commence his new role as a liaison officer and researcher for the SOE, a position he felt very qualified to do. One of the first things he did was to visit Ludwig to show him the George Cross medal.

"John, this is wonderful. Angel and I, particularly me, know how much you deserve it. I would not be here now." Ludwig was excited and wanted to hear what the king and prime minister had said to him.

John was keen to tell Ludwig what the prime minister had said about him. "Ludwig, this means you will have full support directly from the top when you face the International Court, as I am sure the British government will ask for and plead clemency for you."

Chapter 29

The progress of the Allies had gone according to plan, and heavy bombing of Berlin on 3rd February 1945 demonstrated to the world that it was the beginning of the end for Hitler. He had ensconced himself in his bunker near the chancellery prior to the bombing, and would spend the short time he had to live in and around the heavily fortified building with his mistress. They married in the bunker just weeks prior to their deaths.

Ten days later, the historic German city of Dresden was bombed heavily by the Allies, causing great loss of civilian lives and destruction of much of the ancient buildings. The question has remained to this day that whether it was necessary. The war had almost been won, and the German war machine had virtually collapsed.

When John told Ludwig, he said angrily, "Why have the Allies destroyed such a beautiful city unnecessarily, killing all those people? It defies logic unless it was retribution and revenge. It serves no purpose, John."

"I must agree with you, Ludwig. I can only condemn the actions of the Allies. It is necessary to bomb Berlin, but not Dresden. It is deplorable," replied John.

The Buchenwald concentration camp was liberated by the American forces, and as informed by the prime minister to Mark, so was Bergen-Belsen. The Red Army had liberated all the territories in the East that the Nazis had captured, and the Battle of Berlin was about to gather pace.

The Western Allies, after crossing the Rhine, made the decision to slow the advance on Berlin to allow the Red Army to take the city. It would cause deep divisions later when East Berlin was separated from the West. At the time, it was believed that many thousands of lives would be saved, so the decision was made with the best of intentions by the American supreme commander.

There was some disturbing news for the Von Klauses—Switzerland closed its borders with Germany. Angel, who was now back in Switzerland with her daughter, wondered how this would affect them.

The news on 30th April 1945 was what the world was waiting for the confirmation that 'Hitler was dead'. The fascist leader had committed suicide after finally realising that all was lost, and fearing the same humiliating fate as his fellow fascist counterpart in Italy. With Berlin surrendering the city on 2nd May 1945 to the Russian forces after stubborn resistance, Germany officially and unconditionally surrendered on 8th May, and the war had finally come to an end.

The British nation celebrated their well-earned victory on 8th May 1945, and over a million people watched as the royal family and the prime minister waved from the balcony of Buckingham Palace to an ecstatic crowd.

The Groves family was there, and Mary, excited and enjoying every single moment and trying hard to make herself heard, said, "John, we are so lucky. We have been through so much, and I just cannot believe how it's all turned out in the end."

"Well, we have survived the war. Let's hope we can survive the peace. There are many issues with the Russians over territory, and Ludwig is convinced there is going to be a cold war between the East and West.

"An arms race with terrifying weapons is beginning, and these people here today have no idea," said John, more pessimistic than normal.

"John, you are beginning to scare me."

"Sorry, Mary, let's just enjoy the moment, and I must learn to keep my big mouth shut."

In the Far Eastern theatre of war, the Americans were still facing obstinate resistance by the Japanese forces; however, this concluded with the destruction of Hiroshima on 6th August and then Nagasaki on 9th August 1945 with the dropping of the world's first atomic bombs. Japan finally surrendered on 13th August 1945.

On 19th June 1945, the British Empire began the long process of demobilisation, and John became involved through his work with the SOE and the War Department.

Mary had been promoted to sister, a role she'd been waiting for many years, so more money was available for the family.

James was now eligible to do his national service and was attested to the army, and Mary Anne became engaged to be married. Soon John and Mary would have their home to themselves.

"John, why must you be so pleased that our children are leaving home? I'm quite upset about it," said Mary. John did not say anything but smiled contentedly.

The development of post-war London was frustratingly slow, and bombed sites still remained two years after the war had ended. Almost everywhere, there were corrugated fencing to keep the public and children away from the dangers of unexploded bombs, and buildings just collapsing were a real risk.

Rationing on many food items still prevailed, and it seemed at times that nothing had changed since the occupation by the Nazis. But slowly, new housing was been developed, and Londoners were beginning to see the benefits when vast estates of new homes were being built in new towns outside the capital.

Chapter 30

It was time for justice. The Nuremberg trials held by the Allied forces started on 20th November 1945 and finished on 1st October 1946. Some of the political and military personnel of the Nazi regime, who would have faced trial, had committed suicide, and this included many of the leading Nazis, such as Goering.

Ludwig's defence was that he had cooperated fully with first the Russians, and then the British government, and it was deemed to be unfair that he should face the most serious charges. His trial would be heard at the lesser court under the Control Council Law 10, held by the US military tribunals. There was a strong chance that he could be acquitted or, if found guilty, sentencing would be lesser due to the mitigating circumstances. Ludwig's trial was set for 2nd January 1948.

Angel and Heidi had returned from Switzerland to their beloved home in Baden soon after the surrender of Germany. It was an extremely emotional time for them both. All the servants had survived, and seeing them all again was such a joy. Angel's maid presented her with a magnificent bouquet on behalf of all her staff.

"Welcome back to your home, Countess," the maid said. "We have all missed you so much. When is the master returning to us? It has been so long."

Angel was deeply touched and promised she would never leave the castle again after explaining about Ludwig. "You have all been the most loyal friends to my family, and the master—by the grace of God—will be back with us soon. Thank you, all."

Angel began the process of repatriation to have her sons returned to Germany. Dieter was released from British custody on 1st November 1945 and Hans two weeks later; neither would face trial and did, in fact, return to Baden. Ludwig awaited his trial, and the Von Klauses were optimistic that he would be acquitted.

Angel's dream of having her family together again at the castle was almost a reality. The devoted servants had played their part in maintaining the vast estate while their mistress had been absent, and her gratitude was evident when she rewarded everyone with extra pay and a piece of land, each, on the estate.

The war had left many German families impoverished, including the Von Klauses, and it was going to be difficult to make ends meet. The victorious Allies were seeking reparation though the German economy had collapsed.

How she wished Luds was there with her to shoulder the heavy burden. He always knew what to do in an emergency, but now she would have to be patient and wait until after 2nd January, and the final verdict.

Meanwhile, some of the family silver and paintings had to be sold to collectors to meet the financial demands of running the estate, a decision Angel was forced to take very reluctantly. It was déjà vu, just as it was after the First World War had ended in defeat. Angel turned to Heidi for support and asked her if she was doing the best thing to re-establish their flagging finances.

"Mama, you must do this. Papa would be more upset if you allowed the estate to become derelict and unable to pay the servants' wages. I know you would not have sold his favourite paintings." Heidi was reassuring.

"We may have to sell the chateau in the future, Heidi, but I will not do anything until your papa is back with us, I promise." Angel was happier at having spoken to Heidi, but her sons would need to be told as well when they returned from the chateau after being away skiing.

Chapter 31

John and Mary had been enjoying their new-found fame, and London seemed to be good for them. John had made contact with his old friends, particularly Bill; it seemed a lifetime ago when they had executed their sabotage plan. Bill mentioned that he had spent a difficult time being imprisoned and beaten by the Gestapo for a while ,and then suddenly released and allowed to go back home.

That must have been Ludwig's influence, John thought.

'It was the doodlebugs that I feared most. You never knew where they would land,' Bill said.

"What happened to the others? Did they survive the war?" John asked.

"Not heard anything about them really. I think they may have been frightened to contact me, John," Bill replied.

John explained about being forced to make a propaganda film to him and explained it was the reason for his absence, and Bill, being who he was, showed no recriminations towards anybody, saying, "We in the street are all proud of you, John. Just imagine my old mucker mixing with the royals and the prime minister and winning the George Cross medal."

"How is your wife, Bill?"

"She died last year. It was very sudden, and I didn't know she was ill. So I live alone now and would welcome a visit from you, John, to catch up on old times."

"Really sorry for your loss, Bill, and I will visit you sometime and have a beer with you."

As John left Bill, he realised what a good friend he was and would certainly keep in touch with him in the future. John wanted to find out what happened to the Jacobs family, and he knocked on their door. After an interminable pause, Mrs Jacobs opened it to warmly greet John with a smile.

She said, "John, is it really you? Please come in to see Maurice. We thought you were dead."

"No, I am very much alive as you can see, Mrs Jacobs," John replied as he entered their home.

Maurice Jacobs was sitting in his favourite chair, unable to rise to his feet. "John, forgive me, I cannot walk anymore. It is so good to see you alive and well. It has been a long time."

John was so pleased to see them both alive and knew immediately they had suffered badly due to the Nazis. "Are you able to tell me what happened when you were taken away by the Nazis?" asked John.

Mrs Jacobs put the kettle on to make some tea.

"Is it too painful to remember?"

"No, John, it is good to talk to you about it. They herded us into a lorry like animals going to the slaughter, and after four hours, we arrived in a camp with thousands of other Jews—some we knew from Whitechapel. We had no food except a piece of bread and a half cup of water for days, and we did not know what was going to happen to us," Maurice replied. "The men guarding us were very cruel and sadistic and showed no compassion or kindness. Mrs Jacobs became very ill during this ordeal, and I became paralysed during the eighteen months we were in the camp. I often asked myself what we had done wrong to deserve this treatment. Just as we were about to be sent to another camp in Poland, our guards disappeared suddenly. The British soldiers liberated us, and we were hospitalised. John, so many people died in the camp. I cannot describe all the horrible things that happened to us."

John was upset and said, "The Nazis are paying for their crimes, and the leaders will be executed, Maurice. Have no fear. If you need anything at all, let me know. Mary will look in to see you soon. I am so happy to see you both again."

John left the Jacobs's home feeling very angry, but glad they were still alive. When he returned to his house, John told Mary that he had seen some neighbours and began to update her.

"Bill's wife died, Mary. It was sudden apparently."

"Oh, poor dear, they had been married for a long time," Mary said.

"Oh, and the Jacobs's received terrible treatment at the hands of the Nazis. I told them you would pop in to see them soon.

They need help with shopping but are too proud to ask!" John said.

Mary replied, "Of course, John, I'll go round tomorrow and ask them what they need. I'm so pleased that they survived the camps."

"Well, only just apparently. They are both invalids now, particularly Maurice, and Mrs Jacobs can barely walk—poor thing."

Chapter 32

The year 1948 saw the creation of the welfare state, and the lives of millions would be vastly improved. It was a salvation for many impoverished British people, and better standards of living seemed somehow a reward for the sacrifices the long-suffering public had made during the war. The majority of military forces that fought had been denied a decent standard of living for many years. Some had been in both conflicts and deserved better housing and an improved quality of life.

Free medical treatment for most people was now available by way of the newly established National Health Service. Few could deny the benefits of better care for the sick, which would enhance and prolong the expectancy of life for millions.

Both John and Mary still worried about Angel and Ludwig, but it was now 1948, and the trial would soon be taking place. Ludwig would be sent under guard to Nuremberg very soon. John had asked if he and Mary could accompany Ludwig to Germany, and permission was granted. He also wanted for them to visit Angel and go with her to Nuremberg.

When the time came, they were able to wait outside the courtroom so they could hear the verdict sooner. Ludwig had pleaded not guilty to all four of the indictments against him, following advice from his defence team. The military tribunal reached a verdict of not guilty on three counts but found him guilty on one charge. In summing up, the judge said, "Ludwig Graf Von Klaus, you have been found guilty of the indictment 1. Before your sentencing, do you wish to make a statement to the court?"

"Yes, Your Honour, I do," Ludwig replied, anxious to speak. "Considering the gravity of my crimes against my fellow human beings, I have treated fairly and justly by this court, and will accept any sentence given to me without resentment of any kind. I have never been a Nazi, but I allowed them to persecute and

136

destroy the dignity of millions. I was not aware of the mass killings until it was too late, but as a senior officer, I must accept and share some of the responsibility for not having confronted the Nazi leaders before and after the holocaust. The guilt will be with me for the rest of my life. I was a soldier, and war was my business, so I cannot plead guilty for doing my duty. I was under orders directly from Hitler and obeyed many with a heavy heart. The final order was too much to bear on my conscience, so I refused to comply. A sentence of death was pronounced upon me by Hitler and then my family, whom I have seen only briefly in six years, and I would ask the court to take this into consideration."

"Indictment number 1: Crimes against peace by waging aggressive war against nations and violating international treaties. By verdict of this court, you are hereby sentenced to five years' imprisonment. The court has judged that you have fully cooperated with the Soviet Union and the British government, and having been in custody since 1942, we have been able to take this into account and accept your mitigating circumstances. You are now free to leave this court."

Outside the courtroom, Angel was the first to see Ludwig walking towards her with that wonderful smile he always had when hearing good news. Angel rushed to embrace him, with tears of joy running down her radiant face. Heidi then kissed her father on the cheek and hugged him too, equally joyful to have him back again. Dieter and Hans were more formal and shook Ludwig's hand. They had spent many years imprisoned with him, so had not really missed him so much.

Then he turned to Mary and John and said, "Thank you, both of you, for your support." And then he kissed Mary on the cheek and shook John's hand enthusiastically.

The nightmare was over, and both families returned to Baden. Angel had insisted that they all spend some time together in the castle. The start of 1948 had been fantastic, with both families celebrating a year of hope and freedom.

Chapter 33

During the coming months, the harsh reality of post-war Germany and Britain was now apparent, and the destruction of major cities could now be seen from a different perspective. The days of desperation, just being content to survive each day were gone, and people now looked for solutions for reparation and development.

"Germany will rise again, but in a different way. It will become an economic powerhouse for the good of all European countries. However, one dark cloud hangs over the world. Now that East Berlin and West Berlin are divided, this will lead to great hardship for many nations as communism takes hold.

"The aftermath of the last war is leading us into a cold war, and it will prevail for many years between the Soviet Union and the USA. That will included Britain and the Western Europe," Ludwig explained to Angel.

Angel replied, saying, "You are now sounding like a politician, Luds. I prefer you as a soldier. We cannot solve the problems of Europe, but we can help our own family and household, who depend on us. I have plans, Luds, that will make our financial situation strong again, and I think we should sell the chateau to raise money."

"You do what you have to, my darling. You have my full support. I have plans of my own to raise money as well," replied Ludwig.

Angel apologised to Ludwig for selling some of his family heirlooms, saying, "Luds, I had to raise money to keep the estate going and pay the servants as no other options were available for us."

"I understand, Angel. I would have done exactly the same if I had been here," replied Ludwig.

In London, the Groves family was also taking stock of their situation. John was doing well at the Foreign Office. Mary was still actively nursing and was now at a senior level.

The economy of Britain though, was facing serious problems. The rebuilding of London and some of the provinces would take many years, the loans from America had to be repaid, the cost of the war was high both in human and monetary terms, and the public purse was exhausted.

John knew there would be hard times ahead and his ambitions, to ensure his family would never experience the hardships of many at the beginning of the war when the Nazis occupied Britain, were getting higher each year

"Mary, I know this house has great sentimental value for us both and your parents would never move, but we can now afford a larger house with a garden in a better area. What are your thoughts?" John asked.

"Well, I would love to have a garden to grow fresh vegetables. They are really hard to buy these days, and the shops are not fully stocked, but whereabouts were you thinking?" she replied.

"I would love to be closer to my office in Whitehall, and it would be great to cycle to work, instead of taking the Underground."

"Well, I am interested, but we cannot move too far because of Dad. He has not been well lately, and I need to be near them, John, and my own work!"

"Well, let's give it some more thought later then," concluded John.

Six months passed, and both Mary's parents became unable to look after themselves, so Mary reluctantly had them placed into a care home, while Elizabeth moved into a house with a man she had met at her place of work.

Mary and John were now free to move anywhere, so they chose a house close to where Mary was working at the hospital. It was an old Victorian house with a large garden at the rear. Mary was thrilled she could now grow her own vegetables and have a bathroom inside the house. John was also very happy, as he could cycle to work.

Ludwig's prophesies remained accurate, but now the Cold War had spread to Asia. On 27th June 1950, the forces of the

Democratic People's Republic of Korea attacked the Republic of Korea in the south.

Skirmishes had been frequent before, but this major incident officially fuelled an international crisis between the Soviet Union, which supported North Korea, against a United Nations force under the leadership of the US.

The democracies of the West had feared the spread of communism, and troops from fifteen nations were sent to the war zone south of the 38th parallel. The UN forces were able to drive the North Koreans back and away from Seoul in the south towards the Chinese border, and that brought communist China into the conflict.

Later the hostilities ceased, and an uneasy truce remained, with both countries, technically at war. The underlying effect was to alienate the two ideologies between East and West, leaving Korea still divided indefinitely.

As the United Kingdom was part of the United Nations force, John's work with the Foreign Office became relevant again, and his meteoric rise to British intelligence gave him a high status that even he could not have imagined barely a year ago.

Chapter 34

The last ten years since the start of the Second World War had been the most eventful in the history of the British Isles, and the last vestiges of the old empire were coming to an end. The Indian subcontinent—one of the most important—had been granted independence in 1947, and two years later, the old empire became the Commonwealth of Nations.

A new dawn was about to begin, and with ironic consequences and from the ashes of destruction, defeated Germany and Japan were to rise and become economically two of the most powerful countries in the world.

By 1950 Ludwig had written a bestselling book about his life and it made him wealthy again. Angel had pursued her dream of developing the castle into a plush hotel for wealthy tourists and retained all her servants; she was proud of its enormous success.

John had risen to high office at Whitehall with a possible knighthood in the future, still working with Anthony, Richard and, of course, Gerald Clifton-Jones. John would never forget his brave comrades Mark and Etienne, who was still tirelessly searching for his mother. All three men would meet regularly, remaining close friends. What happened to the wonderfully talented Leni? Well, she did not make any more films after the war; however, she wrote bestselling romantic novels.

Mary was now a matron at the hospital where she had worked and had met John way back in 1918. Sadly, Mary's parents had passed away in the same year, and that had brought such sorrow; she and John became grandparents when Mary Anne gave birth to a boy on 1st November 1950, and that brought joy.

The importance of true friendship can never be underestimated. It must be cherished and nurtured and has all the defining qualities that enhance our short lives. The Groves and Von Klauses came from completely different backgrounds but were able to sustain an enduring relationship throughout a most emotionally and physically demanding period of their truly eventful lives.

What happened to the next generation? Well, that's a secret!